THE CASE OF THE MISSING SKELETON

UNRAVELING DANGER: A NANCY DREW-
INSPIRED ADVENTURE

A SERA CRAVEN MYSTERY

BOOK 3

KATHLEEN GUIRE

CHAPTER
ONE

A HALLOWEEN LESSON

IT WAS A CRISP OCTOBER MORNING. The first rays of sunlight pierced through the fog hovering over Maplewood Community Park. Sam, Isabella, and I strolled past the ancient oak that had stood watch over the park for over a century.

Isabella and I linked arms. As I walked beside Isabella, her dark curls bobbed as she leaned in and chatted excitedly about her costume, her deep brown eyes reflecting her joy. We both had the same warm, rich skin tone from our Colombian roots, which made us stand out in this mostly White neighborhood. Isabella's excitement was almost tangible.

Sam jogged ahead. Sam's fair skin and striking blue eyes were always a bit of a contrast to mine, but his energy and eagerness to dive into the mysteries we uncovered were a perfect match for our group. His tousled hair and quick smile made him seem like he was always up for an adventure, just like me.

We were excited that Mom and Dad had promised we could help and participate in the Halloween party at Maplewood Community Park. We were going to Professor Theodore Harrington's house for the morning. He had promised to teach us some history about Halloween.

Mom wasn't too keen on Halloween. She didn't like all the spooky scary stuff, especially because it could be a trigger for traumatized kids like Isabella and me. We were sisters now but we'd both been adopted from Colombia. With the promise that we'd dress up as non-scary characters, and learn about some of the aspects of the celebration, she'd agreed.

We walked up the wide steps to the professor's porch and he met us at the front door. His frame filled the opening. Professor Theo Harrington reminded me of the photos of Albert Einstein in my history book with wild, white hair that seems to have a mind of its own. He had a kind face, with deep-set, intelligent eyes behind round spectacles that are often perched precariously on the edge of his nose. Although he always wore a suit and bow tie, he chose his ties to match the season. The orange of today's tie must be for pumpkins or Halloween since it was the last week of October.

"Hello young scholars," Professor Theo, as we called him, declared as he opened the door to let us into the large foyer. "Aren't we missing someone?"

As we filed in, I turned my head to see the road. "Mandy's parents are dropping her off."

"Should we have hot chocolate and wait for her?" he

said as he ran his hands through this hair, giving it a mad scientist look. We nodded our heads in agreement and he rang a bell.

His housekeeper, Mrs. Eliza Wainwright, marched to the foyer and joined us. Her salt-and-pepper hair was pinned back in a bun. She wore a crisp, buttoned-up blouse with a long skirt.

"And did you wipe your feet, children?"

Immediately three sets of eyes went to the intricate red and green carpet beneath our feet covering the dark hardwoods. A red maple leaf stuck to my shoe screaming that I didn't wipe my feet. I reached down and pulled at it, stumbling backward as the doorbell rang.

Mrs. Wainright marched past us. She grabbed the offending leaf out of my hand as she passed, "I hope you have learned your lesson. Always wipe your feet."

She opened the door and Mandy stood there smiling.

"You're late," Mrs. Wainright commented crisply. "Well, don't just stand there. Come in and wipe you feet." She held up the maple leaf as if it were evidence of a heinous crime.

Mandy wiped her feet and joined us. We stood in a straight line on the rug, waiting for instructions.

The professor leaned out of the large glass doors of the study, peeking out through the slightly tinted glass. "Eliza, stop badgering the kids and get them some hot chocolate."

He ushered us into his study. Mandy, still shell-shocked from the greeting she received from Mrs. Wainwright. She joined Isabella and me on the window seat.

I could tell she was still in shock by the look on her face. Mandy, with her fair skin and bright blue eyes, was always easy to spot in a group. Her blonde hair was tied back in a no-nonsense ponytail, ready for action. Even though she was a year younger than us, her determination matched ours perfectly, and I could always count on her for a fresh perspective. The three sleuths were together again. Okay there were four of us here. But most of time, Sam didn't want to be labeled a Nancy Drew so I excluded him in when Mandy, Isabella and I named ourselves — The Three Sleuths. We may be here for a lesson on Halloween, but we always seemed to stumble upon a mystery.

Professor Theo was the town historian and a retired professor. He'd dedicated his life to studying the town's history specifically, and any history for that matter.

Sam complained earlier that he didn't need the lesson on Halloween but he loved visiting the professor. All the kids in town did. The professor's house was stuffed with ancient artifacts and other cool stuff. It was the kind of place where every item had a story, and the professor was always ready to share it. The room was the same—a cluttered, cozy mess with bookshelves packed to the brim, relics from another time peeking out from every corner, and the scent of old books and pipe smoke lingering like the mist of the October air. In the corner, a skeleton was propped up, its hollow eyes peering at us as if it had a few secrets of its own to tell.

Mrs Wainwright delivered the hot chocolate on a tray filled with pumpkin and cinnamon donuts. She set it down on the professor's desk, after he shoved some papers aside for her.

She scanned the room and mumbled something under her breath.

"I know Eliza, I promise no one is going to judge your cleaning standards by this study."

"Of course they will," she spat as she exited the room.

The truth is we kids knew despite her strict demeanor, there's a warmth in her hazel eyes, especially when she talks about her late husband, who was a history buff just like the professor. But she could send shivers down a kid's spine and make them feel as if they'd stepped into a strict boarding school where they could do nothing right.

Once we had donuts and hot chocolate in hand, the professor searched the bookshelves, pulling books off and muttering to himself, "No, not that one... that one either..." Before he found the right volume, we were on second donuts and a stack of ten books teetered on the edge of the desk. When gravity took over, and the stack fell, Sam jumped out of his seat, knocking his hot chocolate mug on the floor. The last bit of hot chocolate soaked into the carpet. It soaked in fast, turning the bright oranges and greens into a dark, messy blob. The thick hot chocolate spread out, kind of like how watercolors do on paper, only this was thicker and smelled sweet.

Isabella and I set our mugs and plates down on the window seat as the professor congratulated Sam, "Good save, my boy. Those books are precious."

We dabbed at the hot chocolate. "Don't worry about that children. That will be our little secret."

I don't know how you could keep a messy blob of

hot chocolate a secret from a housekeeper, but we kids threw our napkins in the overflowing trash can and sat back down.

Professor Harrington sat in his leather arm chair, adjusted his glasses, flipping through the pages of the faded reference book.

Clearing his throat, he began, "Ah, yes, Halloween, or as it was originally known, Samhain. You see, my dears, this tradition dates back over two millennia to the ancient Celts, who lived in what is now Ireland, the United Kingdom, and parts of France. They celebrated their new year on November 1st, marking the end of the harvest and the beginning of winter—a time they associated with death."

He paused, his finger tracing a line of text. "The Celts believed that on the night before the new year, October 31st, the veil between the worlds of the living and the dead was at its thinnest. Spirits, both benevolent and malevolent, could cross over into our realm. To protect themselves, they lit massive bonfires and donned costumes, often made of animal heads and skins, to disguise themselves from these wandering souls."

The professor's eyes twinkled as he continued, "Now, as Christianity spread across Europe, the Church sought to replace these pagan festivals with their own holy days. They established All Saints' Day, or All Hallows, on November 1st to honor the saints and martyrs. The evening before became known as All Hallows' Eve, eventually shortened to Halloween."

He leaned in closer, the scent of pipe smoke lingering in the air. "When Irish immigrants brought these traditions to America in the 19th century, Halloween began to evolve into the holiday we know today—more focused on community and less on warding off spirits. Trick-or-treating, pumpkin carving, and costume parties all have roots in these ancient practices, though they've taken on a life of their own over the centuries."

Closing the book with a satisfied smile, the professor added, "So you see, Halloween is a fascinating blend of ancient customs and modern festivities, a celebration that has adapted and survived through the ages. Quite remarkable, don't you think?"

I asked the professor if he could share the "more focused on community and less on warding off spirits. Trick-or-treating, pumpkin carving, and costume parties" with Mom.

The professor set his pipe down."Ahh yes, Clare did say she had reservations about you kids celebrating Halloween and dressing up like ghosts and goblins."

"We're not going to dress up as ghosts," Isabella said.

"And what are you going to dress up as?" he asked as Mrs. Wainwright bustled in and refilled the donut plate. She clucked at the hot chocolate blob on the carpet, but professor waved a hand as if to excuse her.

She tromped out of the room huffing, "It's going to stain."

Now that the professor had finished his lesson, we kids felt free to move around the room and chat. We filled him in on our costume ideas. I was going to break out of my Nancy Drew mold and dress up like Miss Marple, an Agatha Christie character Mom had told me about. Isabella settled on a math teacher, while Mandy was still undecided.

Instead of answering what he was going to dress up as, Sam joined the skeleton in the corner. "Decorating for Halloween are you, professor?"

"No," he chuckled. "I hauled that out of the closet to show you so you wouldn't be afraid of skeletons."

Isabella joined Sam and the skeleton in the corner and held its hand.

"Okay, so I know this is a skeleton, but I'm trying to remember all the bones. Let's see… this one here is the skull, right?" Isabella patted the skull.

The professor clapped his hands. "Yes, that's correct. The skull protects the brain and supports the face."

Mandy and I joined Isabella in the corner with the smiling skeleton. Mandy touched the rib cage. "And this big one here in the middle is the ribcage. It's like a cage for the organs, right?"

"Exactly! It shields the heart and lungs."

I added. "And the one that connects the ribcage to the hips… that's the spine, or vertebrae, isn't it?"

"Correct, Sera! The spine runs down the back and supports the body."

The doorbell rang, intruding on our lesson.

A few seconds later, Josiah peeked in the study. "Hey professor!" He turned to us kids crowded around the skeleton in the corner. "Time to go Sam, Isabella, and Sera. Mom's got lunch ready. Mandy, your Mom is waiting in her car out front."

Josiah, at sixteen, towered over the rest of us with his tall frame and piercing blue eyes. His fair skin and stark blonde hair gave him a much more grown-up air, but he always offered a helping hand or a piece of advice when we needed it most. Even though he was older, he made sure to include us four in his plans and made us feel like equals.

We said our goodbyes to the professor and thanked him for the history lesson. Mrs. Wainwright waved a curt goodbye from the foyer.

As we gathered our things and headed for the door, I glanced back at the professor's study, where the skeleton stood with a silent promise: that as long as we embraced our curiosity and faced our fears head-on, Halloween would be nothing more than a thrilling adventure.

CHAPTER
TWO

A HAUNTING DISCOVERY

SAM, Isabella, Josiah, and I arrived first at Maplewood Community Park to plan out the decorations for the town party. I patted the bumpy and rough bark of the oak tree."Guys, this tree is the perfect spot. It looks kinda spooky, but also really magical. I can totally imagine decorating it with cobwebs and maybe hanging some lanterns from the branches."

Sam added, "It's going to be epic. When the sun starts to set, the whole place feels like it's glowing, and the air gets a bit chilly, which is perfect for Halloween."

Isabella poked at the ground beneath the ancient oak tree instead of helping us plan before Mom and Dad arrived with the boxes."I thought we weren't supposed to be decorating yet. Aren't we supposed wait to do that until tomorrow?"

I turned and glanced at her before surveying the

branches of the oak tree where mom had suggested we hang some orange lights."Yes, that's true."

"What's this, then?" Isabella said as she kneeled in the dirt under the ancient oak tree at the edge of Maplewood Community Park, brushing aside a pile of fallen leaves.

I looked over at Isabella and saw she was digging something white out of the dirt, her fingers trembling with excitement.

"Looks like the hand of a skeleton," I said, my voice catching as I felt a shiver run down my spine.

"It *is* the hand of a skeleton," Isabella said, her eyes wide with a mix of awe and disbelief as she carefully unearthed more of the bones, the ancient oak tree's shadow casting an eerie pattern over the ground. "It might be plastic?"

The leaves around us rustled in the wind, adding to the sense of mystery as we all stared at the skeletal hand now fully exposed. I felt a mixture of fear and exhilaration, the crisp autumn air filling my lungs as I realized we had stumbled upon a real-life mystery. Then a thought struck me, and I couldn't help but laugh.

I nudged Sam with my shoulder."Nice one, Sam. Really funny, trying to scare us."

"It wasn't me, I promise," Sam said.

I joined Isabella on my knees, and so did Sam, and we dug furiously until the hand connected to a wrist, which connected to an elbow, which connected to a shoulder.

"Josiah, come and help us," I called.

"What's going on?" he asked as he jogged across the

park.

I stood and pointed at the mound with the protruding bony hand. "We found a skeleton."

"I thought we weren't decorating until tomorrow," he said as he arrived at the mound of dirt.

"I know, I know. I think it's real." I leaned over and continued to dig.

Josiah chuckled. "Real plastic? A real decoration?"

"No, real, " I answered.

Josiah joined us and dug at a quicker pace than any of us could, shoveling huge armfuls of dirt aside, pulling at the sod and rocks until twenty minutes later we had unearthed an entire skeleton.

I reached in to touch the skull, my fingers trembling with curiosity.

"Don't touch it," Josiah said firmly. "Think like Lemon."

I pulled my hand back like the skeleton was hot lava, my heart pounding in my chest. Lemon was the forensic scientist we'd helped solve a case with on our beach vacation at Isle of Tropics. Her words echoed in my mind: "Always preserve the evidence."

"So you think this person was..." Isabella said, her words trailing off in fear, her eyes wide with a mix of dread and fascination.

"Well, it's a body," Sam said, swallowing hard. "That's for sure. Well, it *was* a body. Now it's a skeleton and not a Halloween decoration."

"But you think this body was murdered?" I wondered, finishing the sentence for Isabella. My voice wavered, the reality of the situation sinking in.

Just then, Mandy ran across the park and joined us,

her face lit up with curiosity until she saw what we were gathered around.

"I thought we weren't decorating yet." She put her hand on her hip, a playful smirk on her face. "Why are you burying something?" She stepped back when revelation dawned, her eyes widening in shock. "Is that a human skeleton?"

"Yeah, it is," Josiah said, his voice serious. "And it's real."

Mandy's playful demeanor vanished, replaced by a mix of horror and intrigue. "Oh my gosh, what are we going to do?" she whispered, glancing around nervously as if the murderer might still be lurking nearby.

I took a deep breath, trying to steady my nerves. "We need to tell someone. The police, maybe? But first, we have to figure out who this is. This could be a huge mystery."

Isabella nodded, her fear giving way to determination. "Just like Nancy Drew," she said, a steely resolve in her eyes. "We'll figure this out, together."

As we stood around the ancient oak, the leaves rustling in the wind and the sun casting long shadows over the skeletal remains, I felt a surge of excitement and fear. This was no prank, no Halloween decoration —this was a real mystery, and it was up to us to solve it.

I stood and brushed the dirt off my plaid pants and said, "Yes, it is. It's a skeleton of a real person, and I think that person was murdered," I said to no one in particular.

"Kids, I think you need to move away from the skeleton."

Professor Theo Harrington said from the other side of the fence.

We kids loved Professor Theo, especially us sleuths because of him being the town historian. His love of history and artifacts combined meant he taught us like he had earlier today. Professor Theo had changed into a brown tweed suit and still wore the orange bow tie. He ran his hand through his white hair which always looked as if he had stuck his finger in a light socket.

"I think we should call the...." he stopped in mid-sentence which was his habit. Dad said the professor was so intelligent that his brain couldn't stop thinking so he often sounded as if he was confused or didn't finish sentences.

We five kids said "police" at the same time.

"Yes, those are the folks...." Professor Theo opened the gate and let himself in the park. "Let me take a look at that." He walked a wide circle around the skeleton we'd unearthed.

Josiah stepped away to call Mom and Dad, and the police but not before warning us kids not to touch the skeleton.

Five minutes later, sirens blared and blue lights flashed their way into the neighborhood. Mom and Dad arrived, followed by Lemon and her dog Rusty.

"I called Lemon," Mom explained. "Thankfully she wasn't out on some FBI job."

"Are you kids okay?" she added.

Sam kicked a clod of dirt with his tennis shoe. "It's a skeleton Mom. How could it hurt us?"

Dad gave Sam "the look" and Josiah patted him on the shoulder.

"What's the problem, Sam? I thought you would think this was cool." I asked.

"I do." Sam kicked another clod. "I don't want the Halloween party to be cancelled because of some old bones we dug up."

I didn't agree with Sam, but I didn't say so.Finding a skeleton was a sleuth's dream. Not only did we have a real skeleton for Halloween, but we had a mystery to solve. Whose body is this? I mentally started taking notes.

Lemon pulled a camera out of her bag and snapped a lens on while Rusty ran around the dig site sniffing for clues.

"Can we help?" I asked. Mandy and Isabella shook their heads in agreement.

Professor Theo offered to hold Lemon's bag while she took photos and muttered under his breath variations of "Could it be? ...No it can't."

We ignored him because you never knew what the professor was thinking until his mind stopped whirring and then he'd say something that made sense.

When an officer arrived at the mound, he motioned for us kids to join him at the pavilion so he could ask us some questions. Mom and Dad came too.

Other officers walked around the park like a bunch of ants on an anthill. Didn't they know they were trampling on evidence?

We told the officer the entire story, including how we thought Sam had placed the skeleton there because he liked to play pranks and we were getting ready to plan out decorations for the Halloween party next week.

"I dug it up," Isabella offered, "cause I thought it was Sam's prank when I saw a bony hand sticking out of the bottom soil."

"You mean top soil," Sam teased.

Isabella still struggled with the English language, having been adopted at Christmas into the Craven family, the year before.

"And I came on the scene when Isabella pointed it out." I said, shaking a clod of dirt from a curl.

The officer's eyebrows popped up to his hairline and he took a quick glance at Mom, probably because I used the right lingo.

Mom smiled and tucked a strand of her blonde hair behind her ear."Sera is a sleuth, like Nancy Drew."

"We three are sleuths" Mandy added, pointing to Isabella and me, and then herself. Sam was too, but only when he felt like it, and he didn't like being called a Nancy Drew.

Mandy was my best friend, just don't tell Isabella, or she'll have what Mom calls a meltdown. Mandy wasn't allowed to talk to me last summer after her parents came and got her in the middle of our vacation at The Isle of Tropics but that's all straightened out now. Dad said he took care of it.

"I think that's enough officer," Dad said, rising to his full height. "The kids have told you all they know. I'm going to take them home now."

As we stood and gathered our things, I turned to see the ant-like officers had wrapped the park in yellow crime scene tape.

"Can't we stay and watch, Dad?" I asked before turning to Josiah. "You can watch us right?"

Josiah was quick to say "yes" to keeping an eye on us, probably because he was interested in the skeleton, not watching us.

"I guess so," Dad answered. Instead of leaving, he and Mom lingered. Curiosity was getting the best of them too. After a few minutes and no new information, they walked home.

"Are they closing the park?" I asked, scanning the playground.

"Yes," Mayor Evelyn Harper said as her heels clacked on the sidewalk as she walked toward us. "I'm afraid we have to close the park kids."

"And that means...." I didn't get to finish because Sam interrupted me with.

"No Halloween party."

"Not unless we solve the case of the missing skeleton." The mayor said, straightening her suit jacket. "The whole town is in an uproar."

"What do you mean missing?" Isabella said, "It's right there." She pointed to where the skeleton had been covered with a tarp.

"What she means," Josiah said, taking over, "is that skeletons are bodies of people. They usually go to a morgue and then are buried in ..."

"Graveyards," Mandy shouted, her eyes wide with excitement as she bounced on the balls of her feet.

Professor Theo nodded, his face lighting up with realization. "Exactly," he said, adjusting his glasses as he leaned forward. "So this skeleton is someone who could have been missing."

I stepped forward, my face serious as I looked at

both of them. "The Case of the Missing Skeleton," I said, filled with resolve.

"A missing person" Professor Theo said, correcting me, as he marched past us. "I've got to get home and find my journals."

THREE

SKELETONS IN THE PARK

"I'M CALLING AN EMERGENCY TOWN MEETING," Mayor Evelyn Harper said to no one in particular. She stood in the middle of the sidewalk studying the scene like a sleuth.

"I got your text," Jim Gains called from the other side of the park. He took ten long strides across the playground and past us while holding up his phone in the air. He could come to the Halloween party as a scarecrow with his red hair sticking up in all directions and his legs that jerked around when he walked.

He turned after passing us and said, "Oh hey, kids. Sera, I should have known you would be here."

"Well, yeah, our house is right up there," Sam said, he was still sulking about the no Halloween party thing.

Before Jim could reply, Mayor Evelyn Harper intercepted him, "FBI agent Jim Gains. I didn't realize this was a federal case."

"I don't know *what* this is, officially, yet," Jim said leaning on the picnic table we kids were sitting at. "I'm just here because Lemon texted me."

Mayor Evelyn Harper smoothed her perfect auburn hair and straightened her suit jacket. "Kids I have known Agent Gains since he was a little boy."

Isabella studied Jim. "He was little?"

"When he was younger, stupid," Sam said.

"That's enough, Sam," Josiah said elbowing him.

I stood and unzipped my jacket. "He's upset because the Halloween party is canceled."

"Oh?" Jim looked surprised. "Lemon said the skeleton is old. This crime scene was contaminated a long time ago. Possibly a century ago."

Mom and Dad had gone home with the provision that Josiah keep an eye on us and we stay at the picnic table.

"Jim, get over here," Lemon called. "Kids, you too."

"Just a minute," Mayor Evelyn Harper said, "You can't have kids tromping all over a crime scene."

Lemon stood and wiped some mud off her face with her hand. "No offense mayor, but thousands of kids have been tromping all over the crime scene for years, and I mean *years*."

Agent Jim ignored the mayor and signaled for us kids to join him as he strode over to the the mound of dirt where Lemon had positioned the skeleton.

"About the town hall meeting," Mayor Evelyn Harper called, "Can you and Lemon present your findings, Agent Gains?"

The mayor hadn't left the sidewalk since she arrived

at the park. Maybe it was because she was wearing heels. Sleuths like me, notice details like that.

Lemon snapped a few more photos before turning to face the mayor, "If you use the evidential method of investigation, you should have the kids who found the body report tonight."

Lemon had taught me that in order to solve a crime, you didn't just need clues like what the mayor was wearing, you needed forensic evidence, and physical evidence. There were more modern ways of getting evidence than Nancy Drew had in her books.

Mayor Evelyn Harper sputtered a few words, "Well... I..."

Agent Jim joined the conversation with,"Mayor, the Halloween party is for the kids, right?"

The mayor stood with her hands at her side like a soldier. "Yes."

"Kat and I came to visit my parents just so Louisa and Edmund can go to that party. These kids want to go too," Agent Jim pointed a bony hand toward us, reminding me of the skeleton with his ultra white skin.

"And...." Mayor Evelyn Harper hesitated, rocking up on the toes of her shoes.

"Mayor, M'am," Josiah stood and approached the mayor. "My siblings and Mandy here volunteered to help decorate for the party. They arrived at the park and found the skeleton."

Mandy, Isabella, Sam, and I joined the mayor on the sidewalk since she didn't seem to want to move.

"I found it," Isabella said, smiling her best cute smile.

"Can you kids get in front of an audience and tell

your story?" the mayor was giving in. I could tell because her face seemed softer and her eyes were smiling.

"I'll coach them," Lemon said, as Rusty joined us on the sidewalk, running circles around us and leaving a trail of muddy paw prints.

The wind picked up and blew a tornado of leaves, whipping our hair up into funny positions. I glanced over at Jim who stood with his hands on his hips and his hair on end because he'd just run his fingers through it. The air smelled of pumpkin spice and chocolate.

"I think the spooky Halloween spirits agree," Sam laughed.

"Hey kids, I brought you some hot chocolate and cookies," Mom yelled as she strolled across the park carrying a picnic basket. "Lemon, I made you a pumpkin spice latte. And for you …" she set the basket down, opened it and handed Rusty a dog treat.

"Clare, can your kids speak at the town hall meeting this evening and share, what did you call that?" The mayor turned to Lemon.

"The evidential method. They're going to share their personal account," Lemon joined us on the sidewalk and Mom handed her a Yeti which smelled like pumpkin spice.

"I don't see why not," Mom said as she pulled a glass container full of peanut butter cookies out of the basket.

"I'll take that," Sam said, grabbing for it.

Sam had a history of eating all the cookies so we girls didn't get any.

"Oh, no you don't. Let's move to the picnic table," Mom suggested. "Why is everyone standing on the sidewalk?"

"The mayor is because her heels will sink in the grass and leaves," I pointed to the mayor's four inch heels.

"Smart kid," Mayor Evelyn Harper said.

Mom promised the mayor she would call Mandy's parents and that we would be at the town hall meeting that evening at six-thirty.

———

At six-thirty I stood in the back of the Town Hall with Mom, Dad, my siblings and Mandy. The mayor stood at the podium, looking like she did at the park, not a hair out of place, perfect rosy red lips, and navy blue power suit. I only knew that last part because Mom had mentioned it.

"And now, we will hear from the brave kids who found the skeleton earlier today," she motioned for us to come up to the front of the Town Hall.

I'd changed into a plaid skirt and sweater. Mom had made Sam change into nicer jeans and a sweater. Isabella let me pick out her clothes so I gave her some plaid pants and a sweater so we would both look like sleuths. Mandy wore a similar outfit.

Josiah opted to stand in the back as we kids went to the front. Isabella spoke first.

"I saw something white sticking out of the dirt under the big oak tree," she said before glancing at Mom who gave her a smile and a nod. "I cleared the leaves from it and dug around it. It looked like a bony hand." She turned to me and I took over.

"We thought it was a trick," I gave Sam a sideways glance, "Sam, my brother likes to play tricks so we thought he buried a plastic skeleton as a joke."

Sam laughed, "That's true, but I didn't this time. It was real." He paused to point to Josiah. "My brother, Josiah helped us dig it up."

Mandy stood beside me, her head bobbing in agreement. She had just opened her mouth to share when a man in the front row stood and said, "You let kids dig at the crime scene?"

The mayor clacked her way up to the podium, "Councilman, I assure you…"

She didn't get to finish her sentence before five more people stood up.

"I can't believe kids are digging up bodies at the park," one yoga-pants-wearing, slim Mom said.

"Maplewood Community Park used to be a safe place for our kids," a woman said, her voice trembling like we were the ones who had buried the skeleton at the park. I couldn't help but roll my eyes a little—if only she knew how hard we worked to figure out what was really going on.

Councilman Victor Langston shot to his feet, his face as red as a tomato. "I'm Victor Langston, and my family founded this town!" he practically yelled, making everyone jump. "My ancestors must be turning in their graves right now!"

"Councilman, we know who you are…" someone muttered, but it got lost in the rising chatter.

That's when Lemon stood up, cool as always, like

she'd stepped straight out of one of my favorite mysteries. "The crime scene, as you call it, wasn't contaminated," she said, her voice calm but firm, like she had everything under control. I always admired how she could command a room with just a few words.

The peace was short-lived. A lady in a plaid skirt and horn-rimmed glasses stood and rose up on tippy toes, like a schoolmarm about to correct a naughty student. She cleared her throat loudly, commanding the attention of the room.

"I've lived in this town for over fifty years," she began, her voice sharp and cutting through the murmurs. "And never in all that time have we had something so... horrifying happen! A skeleton found in our beloved park? It's an absolute disgrace! How do we even know that this isn't some... some kind of cover-up? Who's responsible for this mess? And what else are they hiding from us?"

Her words hung in the air for a moment before the room erupted into a frenzy of shouts and accusations. The meeting spiraled into chaos as people demanded answers, suspicions running wild.

Then everything went crazy. People started yelling over each other, saying they were going to move away because the town wasn't safe anymore, and how kids finding dead bodies was just too much. The noise rose to a fever pitch, and it felt like the walls were closing in on us. My pulse quickened, but I kept reminding myself to stay focused—just like Nancy Drew would in the middle of a mystery.

Dad appeared beside us, his face serious as he led us toward the back door. "We're leaving," he said, his voice low but urgent. "Things are getting out of control."

I glanced back at the crowd and saw the councilman's face turn purple with rage, spit flying from his mouth as he argued with the mayor. It was almost cartoonish, but also kind of scary.

"I guess we didn't save the Halloween party," Sam muttered, his shoulders slumped in defeat. I felt a pang of disappointment, but I knew there was more at stake here than just a party.

"You tried," Dad said, giving Sam a reassuring pat on the back, though it didn't seem to make Sam feel any better.

Suddenly, something cold and wet nudged my arm. I jumped a little, my heart skipped a beat, until I looked down and saw Rusty, Lemon's dog, pressing his nose against me like he knew I needed a distraction.

"Sorry, kids," Lemon said, turning to us with an apologetic smile. Rusty kept nudging me, his tail wagging like he was trying to cheer us up. It kind of worked.

"Rusty is sorry too," Mom added, bending down to give him a gentle pat. I couldn't help but smile at the way Rusty looked up at us, all big brown eyes and wagging tail.

Just as Dad reached for the door, it flew open with a loud creak, and Professor Theo burst in, his wild white hair sticking up like he'd just been electrocuted. His eyes were wide with excitement, and he was clutching an old leather journal like it was a treasure map.

"I found it!" he shouted, his voice cutting through the chaos like a lightning bolt. "I found the journal!"

Everyone froze, the room fell silent as every eye turned to the professor and an old, weathered book in his hand. My heart skipped a beat—this was it. The clue we'd been waiting for. Just like Nancy Drew, I knew we were finally on the verge of solving the mystery. Maybe we could have the Halloween Party after all!

CHAPTER
FOUR

A TOWN IN TURMOIL

DAD PAUSED and our family moved to the back of the Town Hall. Professor Theo ran to the front, his wild hair blown by the air vents, giving him a crazy look.

He stopped and gasped. "I've got it." He waved the leather journal in the air. "I know who the skeleton is."

"Professor, take a breath and calm down," Mayor Evelyn Harper said as she led him to the podium. "Come up here and tell us what you have."

As the professor took the last two steps to the podium, Lemon and Rusty followed. She still had her camera bag slung over her shoulder. Rusty nudged the professor, causing him to teeter on the last step. Lemon reached out to steady him. While he regained his balance he spotted us kids at the back of the Town Hall.

"Kids, I found it…" he stopped talking to motion us to join him on the stage.

I looked to Mom and Dad for permission. Dad

nodded yes and we kids tromped up to the stage again. I glanced warily back and forth at the townspeople who a minute ago had been arguing.

We kids stood in a crooked line on the small stage with Sam and me on either side of the professor. He patted us both on the shoulder clumsily. "These kids unearthed the town's founder…"

Before he could finish the sentence Councilman Langston shot to his feet and rushed the stage. "You have my family's journal."

"I have my family's journal," the professor retorted.

The tension in the room crackled like electricity as Councilman Langston's accusation hung in the air. The townspeople, momentarily hushed, shifted in their seats, sensing the confrontation that was about to explode.

The professor's face flushed with a mixture of indignation and determination. "My family's journal," he repeated, his voice steady despite the tremor in his hands. He lifted the old, leather-bound book slightly, as if to shield it from Langston's piercing gaze.

Langston charged the stage, his footsteps heavy and fast. "That's a lie!" he bellowed, his eyes wild. "You've stolen what's rightfully mine!"

Rusty, sensing the rising tension, moved in front of the professor, his fur bristled and a low growl rumbled from his throat. Langston barely noticed the dog as he lunged forward, his hands reaching for the journal.

The professor stumbled back, but not before Langston's hand clamped down on the book's spine. For a moment, they wrestled over the journal, the professor's frail strength no match for Langston's.

Rusty barked furiously, darting between the men, but Langston kicked at him, missing by inches.

"Get away from him!" Lemon shouted, dropping her camera bag and rushing forward. But Langston had already shoved the professor hard, sending him sprawling against the podium. The old man gasped in pain as the journal slipped from his grasp.

"Stop!" I yelled, but Langston wasn't listening. He clutched the journal to his chest, a triumphant sneer curling his lips.

Rusty, undeterred, launched himself at Langston, his paws landing squarely on the councilman's chest. Langston's eyes widened in shock as the force knocked him off balance. He stumbled backward, his foot catching on the edge of the stage. Time seemed to slow as he flailed, his arms pinwheeling before he toppled off the stage and landed on the floor below with a heavy thud, the journal flying from his grip.

The crowd erupted into gasps and murmurs, but Lemon moved with the precision of a professional. She was at Langston's side in an instant, her FBI-issued gloves already on. With a practiced swipe, she retrieved the fallen journal before he could even reach for it. Holding it aloft, she shot the councilman a steely glance. "This doesn't belong to you," she said, her voice authoritative. She grabbed the journal and hopped back on the stage.

Langston, still sprawled on the floor, glared up at her, his face a mask of fury. But before he could respond, Lemon had already turned her attention back to the professor, offering him a hand to help him to his feet.

The professor accepted her help, wincing as he stood. He looked at us kids, then at the townspeople, who were now watching as if a scary movie was playing right in front of them and they weren't sure how it would end.

"As I was saying," he began, his voice regaining its strength, "these kids unearthed the town's true founder, and with this journal, the truth can finally be told."

"We all know who the town's true founder is, you demented imbecile," Councilman Langston yelled as he righted himself and leaped on the stage. " And it's not your great grandfather no matter what your journal claims." He straightened his tie before lunging for the professor again.

As the chaos unfolded on stage, my heart raced. Every detail seared itself into my memory like one of Nancy Drew's most intense mysteries. My eyes darted from the professor's shaking hands to the wild look in Councilman Langston's eyes, cataloging every clue, every piece of the puzzle falling into place. Sam, always ready to jump into action, edged closer to the professor, his fists clenched like he was preparing for a fight. Isabella's usual calm had shattered; she bit her lip so hard I thought she might draw blood, her eyes wide and worried. Mandy squeezed my hand tightly, her fingers trembling against mine, and I instinctively pulled her closer, trying to shield her from the madness.

We were no longer just kids in this; we were witnesses, and maybe even the ones who could finally unravel the truth.

Dad rushed the stage and ushered us out of there. Lemon followed with Rusty. There was no need for the mayor to call the police. The chief was in the audience. As we loaded into our family's SUV, I watched in horror as the professor and the councilman were led to a police cruiser.

As the blue lights flashed, which I thought were a bit overkill, I mean Sam and I fought like that all the time and no one was really hurt, I asked dad, "So what's going to happen to Professor Theo?"

"And the man who was foaming at the mouth?" Isabella added as she buckled herself in.

"The councilmen is a pompous fool," Mom said as she set her purse down at the feet. "I'm sorry, kids. I just couldn't believe he attacked the professor."

Dad pushed the start button, paused to back the car out of the parking spot and answered."They'll probably be questioned and if the professor doesn't press charges, they'll let them go tonight."

"Oh," I looked back and watched the people exit the the Town Hall, their faces bathed in blue lights, looking confused and terrified.

"What was all that about the town's founder?" Josiah asked.

Dad turned his blinker on and stopped before turning onto Main Street. "The councilman has built his whole career on the fact that his family founded the town in 1901."

I leaned forward. "Dad, why would the professor challenge that?" Or more importantly, I thought to myself, exactly who does he think the skeleton is?

Dad glanced at me in the rearview mirror. "The professor has always held the belief that his great grandfather founded the town. No one really believed him. Maybe he thinks this skeleton provides a credible link to his great grandfather's journal entries."

"Ben, the professor lives alone. He has no one. Can't you pick him up at the police station when they release him?" Mom sipped her water bottle as she waited for Dad to reply.

"Yes, Clare," he said as we turned into our neighborhood. "I'll drop you off and then head to the police station."

"Oh, and Ben, bring him to our house. I want to make him something to eat before he goes home."

Sam leaned over and elbowed me. "Score," he whispered. "We can find out what the professor was trying to tell everyone."

"Exactly what I was thinking," I smiled. "Maybe we can solve The Case of the Missing Skeleton tonight."

"And the party will be back on," Sam answered with his one-track mind.

"What are you guys whispering about," Isabella asked from the back seat.

"Tell you when we get home," I said snuggling into my seat, "but I think we can break this case wide open tonight."

CHAPTER
FIVE

THE MYSTERIOUS JOURNALS

"IT'S BEEN WELL KNOWN for over a century that Victor Langston's family founded the town..." Professor Theo stopped talking and stared out the window while holding a cookie in mid-air.

I was sitting on the ottoman in the family room. Mandy had gone home. Isabella was in our room. Josiah had gone to a friend's house to study. Sam had lost interest after the professor had rambled for the first ten minutes about the town history.

Mom had brought out some cookies after the professor had only picked at the leftover beef stroganoff. I know he only picked at it because Mom had said, "Professor you only picked at that, I'm going to get you some cookies and a cup of coffee," as she snatched the plate from him and took it to the kitchen sink.

Grownups are weird. If I only picked at my dinner, I wouldn't get dessert .

Dad asked,"Can you tell us what was in the journal?"

The professor couldn't read from the journal because Lemon had taken it and bagged it for evidence in *The Case Of The Missing Skeleton*. I'm sure she wanted to see if the entries had anything to do with the skeleton.

"Oh yes," he stood and crumbs trickled down his tweed pants and bounced on the hardwood floor as he recited:

"Journal Entry: October 12, 1899

Today, we took the first true steps toward carving out a new life in these wild, rolling hills of Appalachia. With the air crisp and our spirits high, my dear wife Elspeth, our two bairns, wee Duncan and sweet Maisie, and a few trusted friends set foot on this land, determined to turn it into a place we can proudly call our own. The soil is rich, the rivers sing with promise, and though the forests seem endless, there is a sense that we belong here. Together, we have laid the first stones of what we hope will grow into a thriving town, a haven for our families, and a legacy for those who come after us. May our hands be steady and our hearts steadfast as we build our new home. **—Seamus Harrington"**

"So for all these years, Victor has been saying his ancestors founded the town in 1901 when Seamus arrived in 1899?" Dad said, his eye brows crinkling like angry caterpillars.

"Yes," the professor said. "It's always been a

contentious subject between us. I ran for the town council ten years ago but Victor won on his family's history." The professor patted his suit jacket and added, "I can't seem to find my glasses."

"They're on your head professor," I said.

He chuckled and said, "Oh you're right my dear," as he grabbed them and put them on.

"What does that have to do with the skeleton?" I asked, always being the sleuth.

"Here's the sad part of the story." Professor Theo removed his glasses, grabbed a tissue from the side table and cleaned them. "Two years after this entry, Seamus Harrington went to purchase supplies in the next city over and he never returned."

"So he abandoned his family?" Mom said and then covered her mouth with her hand as if she wished she hadn't said that. "I'm sorry, I didn't mean to…"

The professor put his glasses back on. "It's okay, that's how the story has been told for over a century. That Seamus abandoned his wife and children and left them destitute."

"And the Langstons settled here, named the town, and took credit for it," Dad finished for him, his voice tinged with anger as he folded his arms across his chest.

The professor nodded, his eyes dark with old memories. "Yes, and my family began a cycle of poverty. My father spent his life trying to prove he was someone." His hands clenched into fists at his sides, the knuckles white.

I interrupted, glancing up at him with wide eyes, "But you have a huge house on the edge of the park." I had heard Mom talking about how much she loved that house and how it cost "a pretty penny."

"Yes, Sera, I was the first in my family to finish high school and get a scholarship to college."

"And you majored in history to continue your father's quest?" Mom asked.

Mom and I knew what it was like feel like a nobody. I grew up in an orphanage in Colombia until the Craven's adopted me when I was eleven. Mom grew up in foster care and group homes.

The professor straightened his pumpkin orange bow tie,"Yes, at first. But then I realized not only did I love history, but I enjoyed interacting with the students and seeing them light up with joy when they learned something."

"Like finding a clue," I said jumping from my seat on the ottoman. "That's why you ran into the Town Hall waving the leather journal around."

The professor ran his fingers through his hair. "Yes! I hadn't thought about those journals for thirty years. I'd stopped pursuing my father's quest, as you called it, but when you found the skeleton Sera…'

"You said:

'I've got to get home and find my journals.'

You think the skeleton is Seamus."

"I don't know. A lot of settlers traveled through the mountains and some died and were buried along the way. It could be anyone really."

I understood the professor. He got excited because he found a clue. He wanted to share the information with the town, not get in a fight with Mr. Langston.

The doorbell chimed.

Mom went to answer it. After she opened the door, Rusty barked and his paws clicked on the hardwood as he ran down the hallway to the family room.

Rusty ran to me and nuzzled against my leg.

Lemon rushed in the family room, swinging her camera bag. Her blonde hair glowed in the lamplight. Set set her bag down, slipped out of her pink trench coat, and smoothed her pink cable-knit sweater.

"Someone stole the journal!"

CHAPTER
SIX

SUSPICIONS AND SECRETS

AGENT JIM GAINS' voice echoed off the polished hardwood floors, "What happened?"

Lemon stood near the entryway to the family room, wringing her hands so tightly that her knuckles were nearly as white as her pale face. "I stopped at The Cozy Corner Bookstore to grab a coffee. I left the journal on the front seat." Her voice trembled with disbelief. "I've never lost evidence!"

Dad, his face a mask of concern, furrowed his brow as he asked, "You left your car unlocked?"

"Yes," she whispered, her shoulders slumping as if the weight of her mistake had finally hit her. "I can't believe I did that."

The tension in the air thickened as Agent Jim joined us in the family room, his steps heavy. "I wasn't sure if the journal was evidence, but now I know it is," he said, his eyes scanning the room, taking in the somber atmosphere.

Before anyone could respond, the peace was shattered by the sound of thundering footsteps on the stairs. Sam and Isabella burst into the room.

"What did we miss?" Sam asked, his eyes darting from face to face.

Isabella opened her mouth to speak, but the sudden, frantic pounding on the front door silenced her. The doorbell chimed at the same time, sending a jolt through all of us. Mom's hand trembled as she picked up her phone and checked the door camera. Her voice was tight as she said, "The police."

I followed Dad down the hallway, his jaw tightened as he placed a hand on the door. When he swung it open, Officer Bob stood there, his posture stiff and formal, his face unreadable. "We are looking for Professor Theodore Harrington," the officer said in an official tone that made the air feel heavier.

Dad hesitated, his eyes narrowing. "Robert, come in," he said, though his voice carried a note of wariness. "He's here."

But Officer Bob didn't acknowledge Dad's invitation. Instead, he marched straight down the hallway, his boots clapping against the floor like a drumbeat, and entered the family room with a steely gaze fixed on the professor. "Professor Harrington, you are under arrest for assault on a public official and theft of evidence in a murder investigation."

"What?" The professor stumbled backward, his eyes wide with shock as Officer Bob roughly clicked the handcuffs onto his wrists. The cold metal seemed to steal the color from his face.

Dad's voice erupted with disbelief, his fists clenched at his sides. "What's going on here? He didn't assault anyone. Victor Langston assaulted him!"

The room felt like it was closing in, the walls pressing closer with the weight of confusion and fear. The air buzzed with unspoken questions, the once-warm family room now a stage for an unfolding nightmare.

Mom broke the silence with, "Robert, Ben just picked up the professor at the police station an hour ago."

Instead of responding to Mom, Officer Bob turned to Dad. "Were you at The Cozy Corner forty-five minutes ago?"

"I stopped to pick up Clare's book order on the way home from the police station." Dad's eyes grew wide as he turned to Lemon. "I didn't take the journal, Lemon."

"Of course you didn't," Lemon said.

When Dad mentioned the word "journal," the professor's face lit up. "Journal, why, I have it right here. I put it in my pocket." He flailed around, his hands clasped behind his back.

In the excitement of Lemon's statement, the professor must have forgotten that he had the journal in his pocket. I wish he would have remembered before the cuffs were clamped on his wrists.

Lemon stepped forward and fished in Professor Theo's jacket pocket, pulling out the journal. "Sera, can you grab me a baggie?"

My heart skipped a beat as I unzipped Lemon's

camera bag and pulled out a baggie. Something didn't feel right, and I couldn't shake the uneasy feeling. Why would the mayor be so interested in this journal? What could be in it that made everyone act so strangely? I handed the baggie to Lemon, who slid the journal inside.

"Let him go, Robert," Agent Gains said.

"On whose authority?" Robert asked, standing up to his full height, which was a good six inches shorter than Jim. "The mayor sent me here to retrieve the journal."

"But you said…" I started before Dad interrupted me.

"Sera, let the adults handle this."

My mind raced. Something was super stinky. Officer Bob lied about why the professor was under arrest, and now the mayor was involved? Why did she want the journal? Was it for personal reasons? Did the journal reveal something about her family, or was she trying to stall the investigation?

"On the authority of the FBI," Jim said.

Officer Bob unlocked the handcuffs, and the professor sat down hard in the chair. The doorbell chimed again as the police walked down the hallway to the foyer.

Mom picked up her phone. "It's the mayor."

I shifted on my feet, feeling the tension in the room rise as the officers must have answered the door before Mom or Dad could get there. They returned to the family room, flanking Mayor Evelyn Harper.

The mayor clacked into the room on her heels, exuding confidence. "I'll take that." She reached for the baggie with the journal.

"And?" Lemon said, her voice cool and steady.

"I'll put it in the Town Hall safe for the night."

Lemon hesitated but then handed the journal to the mayor.

"We don't want to lose this again, do we, professor?" the mayor said with a smile. But something in her eyes made me uneasy. When the mayor studied the professor's slumped form, her demeanor softened. She handed the journal back to Lemon and took my place on the ottoman, grasping the professor's hands.

"How are you doing, Theo?" she asked, her voice filled with concern.

I watched them closely, my Nancy Drew- like instincts telling me that this was more than just about a journal. Secrets were swirling around us, and I was determined to uncover them, no matter what.

CHAPTER
SEVEN

CLUES AND CONFUSION

THE NEXT MORNING at the breakfast table, I told Sam and Isabella of my suspicions. Mom had made chocolate chip waffles to cheer us kids up. She always made waffles on Saturday morning, the chocolate chips were an extra treat.

As Sam scooped up confectionery sugar out of the bowl and dumped it on his waffle, "Do you think the mayor has something to do with this whole thing?" He waved the spoon in an ark over the table sprinkling snow-like sugar over the waffle plate and cup of forks.

"I was thinking the same thing," I said as I took a fork out of the cup and licked the sugar off before cutting my waffle with it.

"But why would she care about an old journal?" Isabella asked as she sliced her waffle with a pizza cutter. "It wasn't the mayor who stole the journal. It was the professor."

Josiah joined us at the table, forking a stack of three waffles and dropping them on his plate. "The professor didn't steal the journal. It *is* his."

Sam shoved a bite of waffle in his mouth and mumbled,"But he took it out of Lemon's car and …"

Mom entered the dining room with a stack of steaming waffles, set them down, and grabbed the empty plate. "Kids, sometimes Professor Theo gets confused. He didn't steal the journal."

Isabella reached for the maple syrup."He just saw it and thought, that's mine, right Mom?"

"That's right, honey." Mom put a hand on her hip. "I'm going over to check on the professor this morning before my book club meeting."

"We can check on him," I said, a plan quickly forming in my head. We could go to the park, search for any clues, and then go talk to the professor.

"You're welcome to check on him after I do, but you kids have some chores to do this morning."

Mom didn't always understand sleuthing. You had to get to the clues when they were hot, not wait until you picked up your dirty clothes and loaded the dishwasher.

The doorbell chimed. "It's Mandy!" I jumped up from my seat and ran to answer.

I opened the door and before Mandy could say hello, I said, "You're not going to believe what happened last night."

Instead of asking what happened, Mandy said, "We drove past the park on the way here and there is a huge banner over the entrance saying 'Halloween Party,' with the word CANCELED over it."

"What?" Sam yelled from the dining room.

Mom slid past Mandy and me and grabbed her coat and purse from the hooks. "I'm going. Sam and Josiah, you two load the dishwasher," she yelled over her shoulder.

Sam groaned loudly enough for us to hear it in the foyer.

As the door closed behind Mom, I told Mandy our plans. "We're going to the park to look for clues and then visit Professor Theo."

I hung Mandy's coat up on a hook and she followed me to the dining room. Josiah handed her a plate and nudged Sam in the shoulder.

"Oh, yeah," he slammed a waffle on her plate. "Have a waffle."

"I can help you with your chores, so we can go investigate," Mandy said.

"In that case, have some syrup with those waffles." Sam shoved the syrup toward her.

"I'll unload," Josiah said. "You load," he pointed at Sam. 'Don't let Mandy do all your chores."

"Where are you going after chores, Josiah?" I asked.

Josiah stood and picked up his empty plate. "I'm working on a group project for homeschool co-op and I promised the guys we'd meet this morning, squirt."

I wished Josiah was coming with us because even though the skeleton was dead and he wasn't sitting in the park waiting to scare us, I still was a little freaked out about everything. There had been a huge fight at the the Town Hall, the professor had been arrested, and Officer Bob, Dad's friend, had acted like he didn't even know him. Then the mayor came to *our house.*

Things were spooky which meant there was a real mystery here.

I suddenly had a thought. "Are you going to Jed's house, Josiah?" I yelled to Josiah who was unloading the dishwasher.

Josiah paused his chore and stuck his head back in the dining room. "Yes."

Mandy must have read my mind. "Doesn't he live next to the park?"

"He does," Josiah said.

That made me feel a bit better. Maybe we could devise some sort of signal if we got freaked out or found another skeleton. Or worse, Officer Bob or the mayor showed up.

"Can we signal you if we need you?" I asked as I stacked some plates up to help Sam so we could get going.

"Sure squirt," he said. "What's the signal?"

Isabella stood up and said, "How about we yell really loudly?"

"That's a great idea, but that might bring other people to the park including Officer Bob," Josiah said as he ruffled her hair.

"I know," I said. "Isabella can take her GPS watch off. Won't you get an alert on your phone?"

Mom and Dad had purchased GPS watches for Isabella and me because Isabella had run away a few times, an old habit of hers she hadn't gotten over, including last year when she'd gotten kidnapped on purpose. I had one because as Dad said, "sometimes my sleuthing got me into trouble."

"Or you could text me," Josiah said with a chuckle.

"Yeah," I said. He was right I could text him on my watch but it didn't feel as if it fit the mood of the case. Him getting an alert that Isabella was missing was much more ominous then me texting "Help!" But I could work with it.

Josiah chuckled under his breath as he returned to the kitchen to finish his chore.

Half an hour later, after much grumbling on Sam's part and my making Isabella's bed because it was "too hard," we were finally putting coats on to go out the door. I grabbed my pink jacket and backpack with my notebook.

As we walked down the chilly sidewalk toward the park, our breath fogging in the crisp autumn air, Sam's voice dropped to a spooky tone, trying to freak us out with his latest ghost story.

"They said he'd be back before the moon turned red," he began, his words hanging in the air like a mist. "But Seamus vanished, leaving me filled with dread. Now I swear I hear his footsteps on the floor," he paused, glancing over his shoulder as if expecting something to appear, "But when I open the door, there's nothing more."

I felt a slight chill, my fingers tightening around the strap of my backpack. "Did you make that up?" I asked, a mix of curiosity and unease creeping into my voice.

"Yes, it's pretty good, right?" Sam replied, a grin spreading across his face as he kicked a stray pebble down the sidewalk.

"Yes, it sent shivers up my spine," Mandy admitted, rubbing her arms as if trying to shake off the eerie feeling. The wind rustled the leaves overhead, making them whisper secrets we couldn't quite hear.

"Do you think Seamus is glad we found him?" Isabella asked, her voice soft as she gazed at the trees ahead, their branches swaying gently, casting long shadows on the path. Her question hung in the air, and for a moment, it felt like Seamus himself might be listening.

Once we arrived at the park, the sight of the banner with the word "CANCELED" flapping in the cold breeze sent a chill down my spine. It only made me more determined to solve the crime that had cast a shadow over our town. The fog clung to the ancient oak trees like a ghostly shroud, making everything feel just a little more eerie.

"Hey, kids," Lemon's voice floated out from the mist surrounding the ancient oak. I jumped, my heart racing. Rusty suddenly bounded toward us, his dark form emerging from the fog. He greeted each of us with a nudge before circling the swing set three times, as if sensing something was off.

"Don't you think the mayor's actions were a little weird last night?" Lemon asked, her voice low and almost conspiratorial. As I stepped closer, her form gradually materialized, first the bright pink Crocs boots, then her plaid pants, topped with a sweater and matching pink coat. She looked out of place in the dreary fog, a splash of color against the grayness.

"Yes," I said, my voice a bit shaky. "I thought something was weird," I echoed, feeling a strange unease settle in my chest.

Lemon's eyes narrowed as she leaned in, her voice

dropping even lower. "I wondered if there was some-thing else to it, as if the mayor had 'buried' some of the town's history."

"Buried," Sam repeated with a nervous chuckle, trying to lighten the mood but failing. I could tell he was still spooked by the ghost story he'd made up about Seamus. "Get it? Buried!" He took a step back and tripped over a fallen branch, landing on the damp ground with a thud. The sound echoed spookily in the foggy stillness.

"Like this?" Isabella called from the edge of the woods, her voice tinged with excitement.

"What did you find?" Lemon asked, immediately alert, her hand already reaching for her camera bag.

"It's an old rock with writing on it," Isabella said, struggling to lift a weathered stone that was almost too big for her to manage.

Jealousy flared in me, a bitter twist in my stomach. It was really bugging me that Isabella was finding all the clues in this mystery while I seemed to be coming up empty. What kind of sleuth was I?

Lemon kneeled beside the rock, pulling out a special brush from her kit. She dusted off the dirt with precise strokes, revealing the first letter—an S. My breath caught as the next letter appeared, an E, an A followed by an M. The tension grew with each brushstroke until the final letter was uncovered. U... and then an S.

"Seamus," I whispered, my heart pounding. The name from Sam's ghost story, etched into stone, sent Goosebumps prickled along my skin. The fog seemed to close in around us.

CHAPTER
EIGHT

UNEARTHING THE PAST

"WHAT DID YOU FIND, LEMON?" Mayor Harper's voice said from the fog.

The mayor stepped closer, the sunlight that had broken through illuminated her silver jacket and suit. Instead of wearing her normal high heels, she wore silver rain boots which were now sinking into the mud where we'd dug up the skeleton the day before.

What was she doing here? And more importantly, why hadn't anyone found this headstone before?

"We found Seamus's headstone," Lemon explained, pointing to the rock. "This is the man mentioned in Professor Theo's journal."

The mayor leaned over and studied the rock, careful not to touch it. "His ancestor?"

"Yes," Lemon said. "I took some photos of the journal last night. My hands are a bit muddy and I don't want to take my gloves off." She nodded her head toward her camera bag. "Sera, you know how to turn it on."

I unzipped the camera pocket and pulled the camera out carefully, my hands shaking with excitement over the discovery. I turned on the camera and the screen came to life.

"Read the first section," Lemon commanded.

"Journal Entry: November 3, 1901

I write this with trembling hands and a heart heavy with fear. It has been over two years since Seamus left for the city and never returned. The town has whispered that he abandoned us, but I know the truth, and it is a truth I must now confide in these pages, lest it be lost forever.

Seamus returned to us on a cold, moonless night, his eyes wild with a terror I had never seen in him before. He spoke of a man who had followed him, a man who knew too much, who threatened to take everything from us if Seamus did not comply. I could see the desperation in his eyes, the way his hands shook as he clung to me, begging for forgiveness, for understanding. But there was no time for that. The man came for him, just as he had feared."

I paused and glanced toward the headstone, a million thoughts running through my head. Why hadn't the professor's family seen this entry, and was Seamus murdered and why? "Why hadn't the professor seen this entry?" I asked as I clicked to the next frame.

"I found it tucked away in a hidden pocket in the back of the journal. It's likely they never looked because it blended in so well."

Mandy, Sam, and Isabella sat together on a log

waiting for me to read the next section as if I were reading them a scary bedtime story.

I shifted on my feet, and gripped the camera tighter as I read the next section to myself. "Read it aloud Sera," the mayor prodded.

I glanced up to see her face mottled and red. I'd seen that look on Mom's face before when she was angry that someone had been lying to her.

"Yes, please," Sam yelled.

"I heard the struggle from the bedroom, the sound of bodies hitting the floor, the sickening thud that followed. By the time I reached the parlor, it was too late. Seamus lay still, his life snuffed out too early. The man was gone, vanished into the night, leaving me alone with Seamus's lifeless body and a burden too great to bear."

I almost dropped the camera, my hands trembling with shock. "Seamus was murdered!" I gasped, my voice barely above a whisper as the revelation hit me like a cold gust of wind.

"And the professor doesn't know!" Sam exclaimed, his eyes wide with realization.

The mayor's face flushed with a mix of guilt and determination. "I've been a fool," she muttered, her voice thick with regret. She stomped off toward the fence of the park, her boots slipping in the wet leaves beneath her feet.

"Where are you going?" Lemon yelled after her, concern lacing her voice as she watched the mayor march away.

"To talk to Professor Theo and apologize," the

mayor called back over her shoulder, her voice firm with resolve, though a trace of emotion lingered in her words.

Lemon quickly turned her attention back to the task at hand. "Let me bag this headstone, and we'll come with you," she said, her tone brisk as she carefully placed the stone into a large evidence bag. Isabella, always quick on her feet, had already jumped up to retrieve the evidence bag from the backpack. A flicker of irritation sparked within me—why did Isabella always manage to find and do things before I could? But the excitement of sharing this new, crucial information with the professor soon overpowered my annoyance.

"I'll carry your bag, Lemon," Sam offered, eager to help as he reached for the camera bag.

We all tromped through the brown and yellow leaves toward the professor's house, our footsteps crunching in unison. Mandy, ever the considerate one, opened the gate for the mayor, who pushed through without hesitation. We kids followed in a tight line, like ducklings in a row, our anticipation growing with each step. Lemon, bringing up the rear, carefully cradled the ancient headstone as if it were made of glass. Dad would've said we looked like a strange procession, but we were on a mission, and nothing was going to stop us now.

The mayor rang the doorbell. We made a straight line of humans on the front porch while we waited.

"What are you guys doing?" Josiah asked while taking two steps at a time up the porch. "Sera, you were supposed to text me if you..." he stopped as he caught sight of the huge rock in Lemon's arms. "Is that what I think it is?"

"It's a foot stone. I found it." Isabella answered, her hand on her hip.

"Headstone," Sam said with a grin. Thankfully he didn't say it in a mocking tone, like he usually did.

"Let me take that for you, Lemon," Josiah reached forward with both arms.

"Thank you, just be careful..."

"It's evidence in a murder," I cut her off. I couldn't help myself, I had to be part of this investigation one way or another.

Josiah's eyes grew wide as he took the rock.

The door swung open and Mom stared at us with surprise before standing aside and calling to the professor, "Professor Theo, you have visitors."

The gang of gravestone deliverers stopped in the foyer to remove our muddy boots, before joining the professor in his study.

As I stepped into Professor Harrington's study, I immediately noticed something was different. The room was the same—a cluttered, cozy mess with bookshelves packed to the brim and the scent of old books and pipe smoke hanging in the air—but the professor wasn't his usual cheerful self. Instead, he was slumped in a leather armchair near the corner, looking really down. His wild, white hair was just as crazy as ever, sticking out in every direction, and today he wore a bright orange bow tie with little pumpkins on it. It looked like he had grabbed it without thinking, like he didn't care if it matched his rumpled brown tweed jacket or not.

"I'll make some coffee and hot chocolate," Mom said. "Don't start whatever this is without me," she eyed the headstone again before turning and walking to the kitchen.

I handed Lemon her camera and followed Mom.

"I thought you were going to book club," I said as we rounded the corner to the kitchen.

"I was," she said. "Professor Theo was so upset over last night's events, I couldn't leave him. Plus he needed some groceries."

"Where is Mrs. Wainwright?" I asked. Didn't house-keepers take care of grocery shopping?

"Mrs. Wainwright's sister fell and broke her hip last night, so she went to help her today." Mom answered.

Five grocery bags from Joe's Corner Grocery sat on the counter as evidence of Mom's shopping.

"You went shopping?" I reached in a bag and pulled out a Bea's Bakery bag. "And you stopped at the bakery too?"

She paused, the coffee carafe in mid-air. "Well Bea's Bakery is across the street from The Cozy Corner Bookstore."

"And Miss Bea has security cameras," I finished for her.

"Yes," she said sheepishly.

"Mom, you were sleuthing!"

"Yes, I was," she laughed. "I wanted to prove that the professor didn't steal his journal from Lemon's car."

As I helped her put away groceries I asked, "I thought you were going to make coffee and hot chocolate."

She pointed to the carafe she'd held only moments before. "Zoe at The Cozy Corner, fixed up some for us."

"So you went inside The Cozy Corner too?" As I slid two cans of soup into the cabinet, I had to admit she'd done a great job sleuthing today. Then I turned and asked "How did you get all this shopping done?"

"Oh, Joe delivered the groceries. The rest I picked up on my own," she smiled. "How about I tell you the rest of what I found out after we serve these muffins, hot chocolate, and coffee?"

She loaded the tray with mismatched mugs from the cabinet, one which read Joe's Corner Grocery, another advertised Bea's Bakery, and third Cozy Corner Bookstore and Cafe with a stack of red, green, and yellow books.

"The professor has a lot of local business mugs," I commented as I arranged the mugs on a plate.

"Yes, he is well loved in the community. I'm sure these were gifts." She picked up the tray and I followed her with the muffins.

The mayor and Lemon had pulled chairs close to the professor. The mayor clasped both his hands and whispered to him. The headstone sat on the massive walnut desk. Sam, Josiah, Mandy, and Isabella sat on the window seat.

"Did you make the muffins from scratch?" Sam said with impatience. "We want to read the next clue."

"Saammmm," Mom said with warning look as she set the tray down on an end table. I did the same with the plate of muffins.

"We filled the professor and Josiah in on what we found at the park and read the first two sections,"

Lemon explained, her voice steady despite the tension in the room.

"I have some news as well," Mom said, her expression serious, but she nodded toward me. "But you first."

Lemon handed me the camera. "Sera, read the last section," she urged, her eyes fixed on me with an intensity that made my heart race.

Taking a deep breath, I began to read, my voice trembling as the weight of Elsbeth's words sank in.

"I knew what I had to do. For the sake of our bairns, for the sake of the town Seamus had given everything to build, I could not let the truth be known. I carried him to the oak tree, the one he had loved so dearly, where we had planned to lay the foundations of our future. I dug with my bare hands, tears streaming down my face, until the earth swallowed him whole. I prayed for forgiveness, for strength, for the courage to keep this secret until the day I die.

I write this now, not to seek absolution, but to ensure that the truth is not forgotten. Seamus Harrington did not abandon us; he was taken from us, and I did what I had to do to protect our family, our town, and the legacy he fought so hard to build. May this secret rest with me beneath the oak, until the day comes when the truth can be told without fear.

—Elsbeth Harrington"

When I finished, the room fell into a heavy silence. I looked up at the professor, his face pale and his eyes brimming with tears that spilled over, trailing down his cheeks. He didn't wipe them away, his hands trembling at his sides.

"We weren't abandoned after all," he said, his voice breaking with emotion. "Seamus was murdered… and all these years, we never knew."

The reality of it hit us all like a tidal wave—Seamus hadn't just disappeared, he had been killed, and his wife had buried the truth along with his body. The weight of that secret, hidden for over a century, now hung in the air, thick and suffocating.

CHAPTER NINE

THE MAYOR'S HIDDEN AGENDA

THE MAYOR WAS ACTING REALLY weird as if she had done something wrong. I overheard Lemon whisper to Mom in the kitchen when we were grabbing some more muffins, "Mayor Evelyn is spending a great deal of time apologizing."

"For good reason. I have evidence from Bea's Bakery security cameras that could land the mayor in jail," Mom answered.

As we all three walked back to the study with a fresh plate of muffins, Mom stopped in the hallway and pulled out her phone. The doorbell rang interrupting whatever evidence Mom had to show Lemon.

Mom handed the coffee carafe she was carrying to me and went to answer. She swung the door open and Agent Jim Gains' frame filled it.

"What've you got?" he asked. Once he opened the door a little wider, two children slipped in with matching flaming red hair. Edmund and Louisa. Jim and his wife Kat had adopted the siblings after the *America's Future Case* but they were both dead ringers for Jim (dad's words).

Edmund and Louisa had muffins and napkins in hand and were heading into the study with Mom when Jim stepped inside. I peered out to the porch. "Where is Kat?"

Kat and I had worked together on *The Case of The Missing Teen* when we were on vacation at the Isle of Tropics.

"She stopped at the library to see her former coworkers. She'll be here soon." Jim smiled and in two long strides he was in the study, telling Edmund and Louisa to sit while eating their muffins. Both complied and joined Mandy, Sam, and Isabella on the window seat. I opted for standing near Mom so I could see the evidence she was about to show Lemon on the phone.

The rock looked different after Lemon, the forensic photographer, had carefully cleaned it. What had once been a dirt-covered, mossy stone was now more defined, the rough edges and uneven surface clear to see. The letters etched into it, though still crude and jagged, were now more readable. "Seamus" was carved with a rough hand, each letter deep and stark against the stone's weathered surface. The rock had a cold, ancient feel to it, like it had been holding onto its secret for a very long time.

Jim Gains, the FBI agent, was kneeling beside the rock, his expression serious as he examined the etching. His gloved fingers traced the letters slowly, as if trying to piece together the story behind them. Sera stood nearby, her curiosity getting the better of her.

"What do you think it means, Agent Gains?" she asked, trying to keep her voice steady.

Jim glanced up at her, his face thoughtful. "It's definitely a grave marker, but not a professional one. This was made by someone who either didn't have the right tools or was in a hurry."

"Do you think it was the professor's great grandfather?" Sera pressed, her mind racing with possibilities.

Jim looked back at the rock, his brow furrowed. "It's possible. Whoever did this wanted to make sure Seamus was remembered, even if they couldn't give him a proper burial."

"According to the journal, it is most likely Professor Theo's great grandfather." Lemon shoved her camera in Agent Jim's direction and he scrolled through the journal entries.

"There's one more thing and I'm not sure I should show this in front of the kids. Maybe we go to the living room," Lemon held up her phone. "Mayor, could you join us?"

The mayor rose from where she'd been kneeling beside the professor. She tried to maintain her composure, but the corners of her mouth twitched, betraying her panic. The mayor's usually commanding posture slumped, and for a moment, she seemed smaller.

Darn. We weren't even going to get to see whatever Mom had on her phone.

"Keep an eye on Louisa and Edmund while we are gone," Mom said over her shoulder.

The professor had wiped his tears away and was his

usual cheery self. He rose to help Edmund thread a piece of typing paper into the old typewriter on his desk. Edmund plunked away on it, spelling his name while reciting it out loud.

Louisa and Isabella played Miss Mary Mac. They seemed to be on the same wave length, even though Isabella was five years older than her. Josiah studied his phone while Sam, Mandy, and I drifted toward the doors of the study.

I pressed my face close to the large glass doors of the study, peeking out through the slightly tinted glass. The doors were so tall that I had to tilt my head back to see the top, and they felt almost like a giant's doors compared to me. The wood framing them was dark and shiny, and when I touched it, it felt smooth and cool under my fingers.

Sam said, "I wonder what they're talking about."

"Mom has some footage on her phone from Bea's security cameras at the bakery," I explained.

Mandy placed a hand on the brass handle. "Did the mayor do something wrong?"

When she said the word "mayor", the professor's memory must have been triggered.

"Evelyn gave me the journal back."

We three turned at the statement in surprise.

He smiled, his eyes twinkling. "She knew it was mine. I was waiting for Ben to come out of The Cozy Corner with Clare's book order and I got antsy so I got out of the car. I was walking up and down the sidewalk when I saw her."

"She took it from Lemon's car?" I asked.

"I don't know," he said. "All I know is she gave it to

me, I put it in my pocket and forgot about it until Officer Bob showed up at Clare and Ben's house."

When he finished his explanation of what happened, we once again heard the all too familiar trill of the siren shrieking its way into the neighborhood. Who called the police? It must have been one of the grown-ups.

The officer knocked on door instead of ringing the doorbell. From our place behind the study's glass doors, we saw a blurry figure of Jim exit the living room and open the front door with his phone in hand.

This time Officer Bob came for the mayor, not the professor. He led her away in handcuffs.

"What happened Lemon?" I asked as she rejoined us in the study.

"When Mayor Evelyn Harper realized that Clare had the security tape proving she stole the journal from my car, her eyes widened in shock, darting around as if searching for an escape or a way to deny what she knew was irrefutable evidence."

"So the mayor is going to jail?" Sam said, watching Officer Bob guide the mayor to the cruiser.

Mandy and I joined him at the window overlooking the street. The confident, authoritative figure that everyone in town knew was gone, replaced by a vulnerable, desperate woman who had just been caught in the act.

"But why?" I asked.

Lemon sighed, her eyes narrowing thoughtfully as she looked around the study. "The mayor was trying to protect something—something she didn't want anyone to find out," she said, her voice low and serious. "But the past has a way of catching up with you, no matter how hard you try to bury it."

Sam glanced at me, his brow furrowed. "So, what do we do now?"

Lemon met his gaze, determination sparking in her eyes. "We're going to have to examine the past to figure out what's really going on here. The answers are buried, maybe even literally, and we need to dig them up."

Mandy's eyes widened. "You mean like...in a graveyard?"

Lemon nodded slowly. "Exactly. We're going to the town library to find out more about the history of this place, and then we're heading to the cemetery. There are secrets hidden in both, and if we're going to solve this mystery, we need to uncover them."

A tingling sensation crept up my spine at the thought of creeping through the graveyard at night, but I knew Lemon was right. The skeleton, the journal, the mayor—it was all connected. And if we wanted to find out the truth, we had to be ready to face whatever the past was hiding.

CHAPTER
TEN

A RACE AGAINST TIME

IT WAS SHORTLY after lunchtime that Lemon picked me up to drive to the town's old graveyard, so we didn't creep through a graveyard at night. Sam and Isabella decided to stay home. Mandy had a dentist appointment.

In broad daylight, the graveyard wasn't as spooky. There wasn't a full moon hanging low in the sky, or fog sitting on the gravestones, giving everything a creepy feel. It was a warm October day. I'd taken my jacket off and left it in the car after the quick two mile ride to the graveyard.

"What are we looking for Lemon?" I swung my backpack over my shoulder and looped both arms through so I could help Lemon carry her equipment.

Rusty jumped from the back when Lemon opened the hatch and he sniffed around the first few gravestones. Lemon called him over and snapped a leash on him. "No digging for bones here, boy."

Then she added, "I have a map of the cemetery." She pulled it out of her pocket and shoved it toward me. "You manage the map and I'll carry my camera bag. We're looking for two families – the professor's – Harringtons and the councilman's - Langstons.

"Why the Langstons?" I knew why we were looking for the professor's.

"Victor Langston claims his family founded the town in 1901 and it seems to be true evidenced by the records in the library and probably the graveyard. I want to check the dates and see how the professor's family compares."

I studied the map. "The Langston family should be straight ahead, in the center of the cemetery. The professor's family has a small plot at the back of the cemetery. It looks as if the Langstons have a monument."

Lemon and I stood in front of the Langston family monument, the imposing obelisk casting a long shadow over us. I couldn't help but feel small in its presence.

"It's huge," I said, craning my neck to take in the full height of the monument. "I've never seen anything like it."

Lemon nodded, her eyes scanning the intricate carvings along the sides. "It's meant to be impressive. A monument like this isn't just about remembering the dead; it's about reminding everyone who's in charge— even from the grave."

I ran my fingers over the cold, smooth surface of the base where the name "Langston" was boldly engraved. The letters were deep, precise, and unyielding, just like the family it represented. "They really wanted everyone to know they were important, didn't they?"

"Absolutely," Lemon replied, adjusting her camera bag. "This monument is a statement. It says, 'We built this town, and we'll be remembered for it.' Look at the way the headstones are arranged around it, like sentinels guarding their legacy."

I glanced at the meticulously maintained headstones, each one standing tall and proud, just like the monument they surrounded. The epitaphs were detailed, recounting the lives and accomplishments of the Langston family members, as if to prove their worth to anyone who dared question it.

"But does this mean they really did found the town?" I asked, my curiosity bubbling to the surface. "Or is this just them making sure everyone believes it?"

Lemon tilted her head, considering my question. "That's the thing about history, Sera. It's often written by those who have the power to tell the story. This monument, these headstones—they're all part of the narrative the Langstons wanted people to believe. But that doesn't mean it's the whole truth."

I frowned, thinking about the small plot at the back of the cemetery where Professor Harrington's family rested. There was no grand monument there, just simple headstones that seemed almost forgotten in comparison.

"Do you think the professor's family really founded the town?" I asked, my voice quiet.

Lemon looked at me, her expression thoughtful. "It's possible. But proving it might be harder than you think. The Langstons have had over a century to cement their story, and this monument is a big part of that. But sometimes, the truth is buried deeper than we realize. It's up to us to dig it out."

I nodded, feeling a mixture of determination and uncertainty. "Then we better start digging."

Lemon smiled, her eyes twinkling with a hint of mischief. "I like the way you think, kid. Let's see if we can find out what the Langstons are really hiding."

Of course, we weren't literally digging up the graves. Our digging would take place at the local library. First, Lemon wanted to snap photos of the headstones and we planned to create a timeline with the dates.

I followed Lemon as we made our way to the back of the cemetery, the air growing cooler and more still with each step. The towering form of the Langston monument loomed in the distance, but as we approached the Harrington plot, it felt like we were entering a different world entirely.

"Is this really it?" I asked, my voice tinged with disbelief. The plot was small and tucked away, almost as if it had been forgotten. The grass was uneven, dotted with patches of wildflowers and weeds that seemed to have claimed the space as their own.

Lemon sighed, her eyes scanning the area. "Yeah, this is it. Not exactly what you'd expect from a family that might have founded the town, huh?"

I kneeled down beside one of the headstones, its surface rough and worn from years of neglect. The name "Harrington" was barely legible, the letters eroded by time and weather. A faint smell of damp earth hung in the air, mixing with the sweet scent of the wildflowers that had taken root around the graves.

"This is…sad," I murmured, tracing the outline of a faded date with my finger. The stone was cool to the touch, almost like it was pulling the warmth from my hand. "It's like they've been forgotten. There's nothing grand or important here—just these old, crumbling stones."

Lemon crouched beside me, her face serious. "It's definitely a far cry from the Langston monument, that's for sure. No one's taking care of this plot, and it shows. But it makes you wonder, doesn't it?"

I looked up at her, confused. "Wonder what?"

"Why a family that might have founded the town would end up with such a puny, unkept plot," Lemon replied, brushing some loose dirt from the base of one of the stones. "If they were really the town's founders, shouldn't they have something more…grand? Something that would make people remember?"

I nodded, feeling a strange mix of frustration and sadness. The plot was so small, compared to the Langstons' grand display. It was hard to believe that this could belong to a family as important as the professor claimed.

"It doesn't make sense," I said, my voice rising with disbelief. "If the Harringtons were so important, why wouldn't they have a monument like the Langstons? Why would they be buried back here, like they don't matter?"

Lemon's eyes softened as she looked at me. "Maybe because they didn't care about being remembered that way. Or maybe because someone else wanted to make sure they weren't remembered at all."

The wind rustled through the trees, sending a shiver down my spine. I couldn't shake the feeling that something was wrong, that there was more to the story than we were seeing.

"We have to figure this out," I said, standing up and brushing the dirt from my hands. "We can't let the Langstons be the only ones telling the town's history."

Lemon smiled, a glint of determination in her eyes. "You're right, Sera. It's time to uncover the truth—and make sure the real founders get the recognition they deserve."

As we walked away from the Harrington plot, I couldn't help but glance back at the old, neglected stones. They might have been small and unkept, but I knew there was more to the story. And I was determined to find out what it was.

CHAPTER
ELEVEN

A MIDNIGHT SEARCH

AFTER LEMON DROPPED me off at home, I spent the last bit of the afternoon constructing at time-line for the Langstons and Harringtons. I got the white-board out of the closet and wrote in the dates and names:

Combined Family Timeline

1850: Jonathan Langston is born.

1860: Margaret Langston is born.

1871: Seamus Harrington is born.

1878: Victor Langston is born.

1880: Eleanor Langston is born.

1881: Elsbeth Harrington is born.

1896: Duncan Harrington (son of Seamus and Elsbeth) is born.

1899: Maisie Harrington (daughter of Seamus and Elsbeth) is born.

1901: Seamus Harrington dies.

1905: Robert Langston (son of Victor and Eleanor) is born.

1910: Jonathan Langston dies. Mary Langston (wife of Robert) is born.

1921: Samuel Harrington (grandson of Seamus and Elsbeth, son of Duncan) is born.

1945: Victor Langston (father of Robert) dies.

1950: Eleanor Langston dies.

1951: Elsbeth Harrington dies.

1976: Duncan Harrington dies.

1980: Robert Langston dies. Victor Langston (son of Robert) is born.

1982: Maisie Harrington dies.

1985: Mary Langston dies.

2000: Samuel Harrington dies.

I wanted to see them side by side. Truth is, I didn't invite anyone in because Isabella had been scooping me on too many clues. If I invited Isabella, Sam would come. Of course, Isabella could come in at any time since we shared a room. Sam had been playing video games in a funk when I got home because according to the local news dad followed, the Halloween party was still canceled.

Once I had all the dates on the board, I wasn't sure what to do next. Elsbeth Harrington and Jonathan Langston were alive and lived in the town at the same time.

I was just trying to figure out how to do the research when Isabella stumbled into the room. "Oh, there are two Victor Langstons, but one is deceased. If he was still alive he would be one hundred and forty-six." She put her hand over her mouth and laughed.

Since Isabella had adjusted more to being part of the family, her raging meltdowns had been much fewer and an amazing thing had happened. She got smart. Really smart. And as much as I hated to admit it, smarter than me. And it rubbed me the wrong way.

I stuffed the angry green monster of jealousy down for the moment and decided to use Isabella's gifts. "How can we do some more research on these names without going to the library?"

"What about the internets?"

With all her smarts, Isabella still confused words which made me giggle.

I threw my whiteboard marker down. "Yes!"

"I'm an intelligence, right?" She twirled around the room and plopped on her bed.

I stood and opened the bedroom door. "I'll go ask Josiah."

Isabella stood up and followed.

Josiah was in his room working on the group project. His laptop was propped open on the bed while he sat on the floor gluing graphs on a project board. He huffed, "I can't get these straight!"

"Maybe this isn't the best time to ask for help?" Isabella and I backed up and hovered in the doorway.

He removed the glue from his fingers with a wipe. "What do you need, squirt?"

I took a step forward and picked up a graph. "We need to do some research on the Langston and Harrington families."

He reached for the paper."Don't mess with that Sera, that's for my project."

I handed it to him and glanced at the title in block words -

"Tracing the Roots: A Historical Analysis of Maplewood's Growth"

I leaned over and examined the papers he was trying to glue to the board. "What are these graphs?"

"Oh, those are histograms." Josiah stood as if he were presenting to a panel of judges.

"Okay, so for the age distribution part, I made this graph that shows how old people were in our town at different times, like in 1900 and then again in 1950 and 2000. You can see whether the town had more kids, more adults, or more older people at each of those times. It's kinda cool because you can tell if the population was getting older, like maybe people were living longer, or if the town was having a baby boom and getting younger."

Isabella's eyes widened with interest and she leaned in, her eyes scanning the graphs. "That's interesting. So what about money? Do you do that too?"

Josiah held up a blue, yellow, and red bar chart. "Yes, check this out— for the economic class distribution, I made this histogram that shows how much money people were making in different decades. It's awesome because you can actually see if most people were, like, super rich, middle class, or having a tough time. It really shows whether the town was getting wealthier over time or if the gap between the rich and poor was growing. It's crazy to see the changes laid out like this!"

"Wow," Isabella plopped down on the floor and examined the rest of the project. "I could help you with this."

I joined Isabella on the floor and I picked up an image and studied it.

Josiah chuckled."As much as I'd love to share my project with you, there's a reason you two came in here."

"What's this?" I asked instead of answering him.

"Oh that's the town crest," Josiah answered.

"Why isn't it posted in the Town Hall?" I asked, waving the paper around.

"Stop waving that around. And to answer your question, I don't know."

"What's going on?" Sam said, leaning against the doorway of the room.

I ignored him.

"She found a clue," Isabella offered, "I can tell by the crinkles on her forehead."

I stood and paced. "So, the town crest has a big blue shield with a silver dragon on it. Above the shield is a gold crown with a fancy ribbon, and on top of that, there's a small helmet as the crest. There's a banner with the motto 'Always Brave' written on it."

"And…." Sam prodded.

"I've seen this before," I waved my arm around for emphasis.

"Where?" they all three said in unison.

"Elsbeth Harrington's grave stone."

Everyone fell silent and the wind blew a cold blast in the window Josiah had left open. I shuddered.

"Does this mean...?" Sam asked, not finishing his sentence.

"We don't know what it means," Josiah said, rising from the floor and gathering his papers. "You wanted my help."

He propped his board up on the desk, "First help me assemble my board."

Isabella grabbed a pair of scissors and took a graph from the desk and while cutting it out said, "Josiah, do you need the birth and death remains of the town?"

"You mean 'records'?" Sam asked as he snatched another pair of scissors from a mug on the desk.

Isabella ignored him. "Sera has them on a whiteboard."

"I'd like to see that. Go grab your whiteboard, squirt," Josiah ruffled my hair.

I was trying to keep my anger and jealousy at Isabella at "an even keel" as dad would say, but here it was bubbling over like a cauldron of witches brew. Not only was she seeing clues I didn't, but now she was ordering me around. I shoved Sam with my shoulder as I exited the room to go across the hallway to mine. I grasped the edge of the whiteboard and pulled it across the hallway. The runner on the floor bunched up and the board got stuck. I looked in the open door. Josiah and Isabella were chatting and gluing graphs on the board. Sam sat cross-legged on the floor snipping with the scissors and humming.

I decided right then and there I was going to solve this mystery on my own. I didn't need Isabella taking over my sleuthing. I didn't need Josiah looking clues up on the internet. I didn't need Sam and his constant teasing. I would go alone to the graveyard and look at the gravestone again. I thought for sure, Elsbeth's grave had a crudely etched carving of the dragon and some of the crest.

"Dinner," Mom yelled from the bottom of the stairs, which saved me from talking to my siblings. I slid the whiteboard into Josiah's room and propped it against the wall.

Josiah set his glue stick down. "Guess we'll have to look at that later, squirt. Let's go eat."

I acted as normal as possible through dinner and the rest of the evening. Then my plan unraveled as I fell asleep on the couch while watching *HOME* with the family. Dad helped me to bed and tucked me in. I waited until he closed the door before I slid out of bed and grabbed my backpack. I checked my watch, eleven-thirty p.m. I'd set aside some black pants and sweatshirt for sleuthing in the graveyard. I changed out of my plaid pants and sweater quietly so as not to wake Isabella.

Once I was dressed, I tiptoed downstairs and sneaked out the front door, hoping Mom wouldn't notice. I could only wish she thought the chime was the raccoon who'd been getting into our trash, wake dad who would roll over and say he'd handle it in the morning. The graveyard was two miles away. I wheeled my bike from the garage before hopping on and coasting down the driveway.

The moon large and bright, hung low in the sky with a mystical and haunting quality. The moon in late October has a way of transforming the familiar into the mysterious. Heading to the graveyard at this time feels like something out of a story, one where the moon is the main character, lighting the way but also making me wonder what might be hiding in the shadows.

It didn't take me long to ride to the graveyard, but once I was there it was as if I'd arrived on another planet. Earlier today, it didn't seem spooky. But now with the clouds drifting by, they shrouded the moon in a ghostly veil, giving it an otherworldly aura that creeped me out.

I parked my bike and reminded myself why I was here. I was going to do a tombstone rubbing of Elsbeth's grave to see if I can make out the town crest I'm sure I saw earlier. I hiked past the Langston monument and hummed to myself as I hurried to the back of the graveyard.

I tripped over a branch and landed on my hands in a pile of mushy leaves, freaking myself out. I stood and wiped my hands on my pants. "You're okay, Sera." I told myself.

Why was I humming the science song, "Dem Bones":

"The head bone's connected to the neck bone,
The neck bone's connected to the shoulder bone…
Now hear the word of the Lord."

To stop myself from totally freaking out, I sang the verse out loud as I trekked the last little bit up the hill.

Once I arrived in the Harrington family plot, I found Elsbeth's grave, set my backpack down and unzipped it. I pulled out my paper, crayons and tiny camping lantern. I turned on the lantern and set it on the wet grass. It lit up the grave but also cast a creepy shadow over my feet.

I placed the paper over the stone and with the crayon, rubbed to capture the crest.

I was almost finished when a twig snapped behind me. I turned to see who or what it was when a voice said from the fog that had settled around me, "What are you doing here?"

CHAPTER
TWELVE

STOLEN EVIDENCE

I JUMPED AS MUCH as you can while you are on your knees. I rolled like a pill bug taking my paper and crayon with me.

"I remembered something else…"

I picked up my mini lantern and held it up to the voice.

Glowing white hair framed by a ghostly white face was attached to a neck wearing a pumpkin bow tie.

He crouched down to help me to a seated position. "Sera, you shouldn't be out here by yourself."

"Professor!" I said gaining my wits. "I found something." I swung the lantern around and it illuminated the headstone. "It's your family crest."

The professor ran his hands over the rough etching on the stone. "That's what I lost."

"What do you mean you lost it?" Sometimes the

professor didn't make sense. It was right here. "Did you know this is the town crest?" I added.

"Yes, yes," he said. "This is one of the original items that Councilman Victor Langston and I argued over. I used it as evidence that my family founded the town."

Now that I knew I was safe, I continued the rubbing. "Why isn't there a replica of it at the Town Hall or in the library or anywhere?"

The professor straightened his bow tie. "After my argument with Councilman Victor Langston in which I took him to this very grave, it disappeared. It was taken down off the walls of the Town Hall and the library."

"Don't you have one?" I asked remembering the stacks of books and papers in his study, plus the maps and old paintings of Scotland lining the walls.

He paced back and forth in his family's plot. "I did. But tonight, I couldn't find it. So I came here."

"Sera Craven," a voice bellowed from the fog.

There was no guessing game needed to figure out who was yelling my name. I glanced at my tracking watch. Foiled by my watch again. Nancy Drew didn't have to mess with modern devices like this. She just snuck off and did her thing and solved the crime.

"Oh, hello Ben," the professor said as Dad stepped through the fog.

"Professor, I hope you didn't bring her here," Dad said, his anger evident in his voice.

The professor pulled his shoulders back and felt for his glasses on top of his head. "Of course not. I asked her what she was doing out here at this time of night."

"I rode my bike, Dad." I stood, my tombstone

rubbing complete. I shoved it toward Dad and the professor, "But look what I found."

Dad pulled his phone out of his sweats pocket and turned on the flashlight. "This is the old town crest. It disappeared about ten years ago."

"It was stolen," Professor Theo said as a twig snapped behind him in the mist.

I jerked around to see who or what was behind us.

The air was thick with tension. The mist curled around my legs, shrouding the gravestones in an eerie glow. Every sound seemed amplified in the stillness—especially the sharp snap of a another twig breaking somewhere behind us.

I froze, my breath catching in my throat as my eyes darted toward the noise. The professor's hand tightened around the lantern, casting flickering shadows across the ancient headstones. Dad took a cautious step forward, his muscles tensed, ready for anything.

Then, we heard it—a soft rustling, the faintest whisper of movement through the dry leaves. I strained my ears, my heart pounding. Suddenly, something darted through the mist, a shadowy blur moving low to the ground.

I gasped, gripping Dad's arm as a chill ran down my spine. The professor held his breath, the lantern light trembling in his grasp. The sound of the movement grew closer, and then it emerged—a sleek, black cat, its fur glossy in the dim light.

The cat paused, its bright green eyes wide and curious as it flicked its tail. It sniffed the air, ears twitching as it took in the scene. The cat's soft purrs and the gentle rustling of its fur against the leaves were a stark contrast to the fearful silence that had gripped them moments before.

Relief washed over me in waves. I let out a breath I didn't realize I was holding, Dad chuckled softly, and even Professor Theo managed a nervous laugh.

"It's just a cat," I said, my voice shaky but relieved.

The cat, seemingly unfazed by its dramatic entrance, stretched lazily before padding away into the darkness. The three of us stood there for a moment longer, the tension broken, as we shared a relieved smile.

"How about we continue this conversation some-where else?" Dad suggested.

"I agree," the professor said as he handed me back the lantern he'd grabbed out of my hand when the cat haunted us.

Dad loaded up my bike in the back of his SUV at the entrance of the graveyard as a police cruiser rolled to a stop beside us.

The driver window rolled down. "Hey, Ben what are you doing here this time of night?"

Dad pushed the button on the hatch and it closed itself slowly. Long enough for Dad to pause before stepping around the SUV and joining Officer Bob at the cruiser window.

Dad leaned over the window, folding his arms on the frame. "So, you're talking to me again?"

"Hey, I'm sorry about that. There are some powerful people in this town who can make life a living...." he paused midsentence and glanced at me before continuing, "difficult."

"Do you mean the mayor who was arrested for theft? Or Victor Langston?" Dad said, straightening and putting his hands on his hips.

Professor Theo shook my crayon drawing in the air . "I'd like to report a theft."

A CHILLING CONFRONTATION

PROFESSOR THEO FILLED Officer Bob in on the theft of the town crest ten years earlier as Bob exited the vehicle.

Officer Bob leaned one elbow on his cruiser with his other hand on his holster"I don't think there's anything I can do about that."

"And why not?" Dad asked.

"Because of what I said a minute ago, Ben." He straightened and continued. "Don't go digging into stuff you don't know anything about. If you know what's good for you, stay out of it."

The professor shook my crayon drawing again."But it was my family crest and it's been removed from everywhere."

"Professor, leave it alone." Officer Bob slid into his cruiser and winked at me.

"Wait," I said lunging for the door. "Why was it removed?"

"Sera, I know you're a Nancy Drew kind of gal, but leave this alone. For your sake, and your family's"

Dad pulled me behind his back protectively. "Are you threatening my family?"

"No, Ben, I'm not. But trust me. You don't want to bother this whole mess," he waved his hand out of the cruiser toward the graveyard.

"You mean the skeleton too?" I said from behind Dad's back.

"Yes, Sera. The skeleton. The history. The family crest." He started the cruiser. "Leave it alone and I can guarantee you kids can have your Halloween Party." Then he sped off down the road.

I knew two things from that conversation. One, we weren't going to stop investigating. And two, we were on to something big. Exactly what it was, I had no idea.

"Dad, what is going on in this town?" I asked as he helped the professor into his car.

"I don't know, Sera. I want to get home and talk about this with your mother, but this is something adults need to handle. Not you." He slammed the professor's driver door shut. "Are you going to be okay, professor?"

The professor started his gold Volvo and nodded. He placed the drawing on the passenger seat and shoved the car into gear. "Why don't the sleuths come visit me tomorrow?" he said to both of us.

"Can we, Dad?"

"As long as you are just visiting, not trying to solve the case," Dad said.

After setting a time, we climbed in the SUV and drove home in silence.

At home, I changed into my PJs and climbed into bed. But my mind wouldn't stop. I climbed back out of bed and pulled my board out into the hallway so Isabella could sleep. I had the dates of births and deaths of the Langston and Harrington families, but why did that matter now? What happened all those years ago that made someone want to murder Seamus Harrington? What was Elsbeth so afraid of that kept her from telling the truth and left her and her family destitute for the rest of her life?

According to the data Josiah had gathered, the contingent of the population who had become increasingly wealthy was Councilman Victor Langston's family and Mayor Evelyn Harper's family.

The thing is, everyone had bad things happen in their family's past, but that was no reason to bury it. Literally. Was it? What secret, if uncovered, would change things now?

With these questions circling in my mind, I finally fell asleep.

"Hey squirt, what are you doing sleeping in the hallway?"

"Oh, Josiah, can I see your notes for your project?"

"In the morning, sure." He helped me to my feet. "It's three o'clock in the morning. Let's get you to bed."

Josiah helped me to bed and tucked me in.

I awoke to the sun shining in the front windows. Isabellas's bed was empty. I grabbed a pair of green plaid pants from my drawer and a matching sweater and dressed quickly. I moved to the bathroom, brushed my teeth, and only then did I check the time. It was ten a.m. I'd really slept in. And we were supposed to be at the professor's at eleven a.m. After washing my face and smoothing my unruly curls with some leave in conditioner, I ran down the steps.

I slowed my pace when I heard Mom and Dad talking in his study.

"Something really strange is going on in this town," Dad whispered loudly.

"Mandy's mom said the mayor is out of jail and has been back in her office like nothing ever happened."

"That doesn't make sense," Dad continued. "Bob was acting really strange last night. He threatened Sera and me."

I couldn't help it. I paused and listened at the crack of the French doors.

"But why would Bob be involved?"

"It's as if Bob, the mayor, and Victor Langston have some sort of agenda. They want the professor discredited."

"What do you mean discredited?" Mom said.

"The professor's house keeper, Eliza, called me this morning…"

Something's wrong—I can feel it. Pressing my ear to the crack in the door, I catch the sound of Dad's voice, low and serious.

"Clare, they took him in today. The professor…Theo…he's been committed for a psych evaluation."

I froze. Professor Theo? Taken in? My mind raced, trying to make sense of what I just heard. Why would they take him?

"What? No, that can't be right. Theo? He's eccentric, sure, but this?"

I press closer to the door, my breath catching in my throat. Professor Theo is eccentric, yeah, but that's what makes him...*him*. He's the smartest person I know, even if he's a little...scattered.

Dad's voice was calm, but there was something under it, something that makes me shiver. "It happened this morning. Officer Bob showed up at his house, said they'd received complaints about his behavior. The mayor was behind it, I'm sure of it. They had him taken in for an evaluation. Said it was for his own good."

My stomach dropped. The mayor? Why would she do this? Professor Theo isn't dangerous—he's kind. He talks to me like I'm not just a kid. What could they possibly be thinking?

Mom was pacing; I could hear the click of her boots on the hardwood. She sounded like she was about to explode.

Mom's voice was sharp "For his own good? Or for theirs? This town doesn't like when people dig too deep. He was getting too close to something, wasn't he?"

My heart pounded in my chest. What did Professor Theo find out? He was always talking about history, about the past, like it was alive. What could be so important that they'd lock him up?

There was a long pause, and then Dad said,"I don't know, Clare. But I'm afraid they're trying to silence him. He's been saying some pretty wild things lately, but...what if he's right? What if they're just trying to discredit him?"

Silence hung in the air, heavy and thick. I could barely breathe. The professor was in trouble, real trouble, and no one was going to help him. Not unless I did something. But what could I do?

I pulled away from the door, my mind spinning. The house was still, but inside, I was anything but. I had to do something—anything. Professor Theo wasn't crazy; he was smart, and he was in danger because of it. I knew I was just a kid, but I couldn't let them get away with this.

As I slipped back upstairs to my room, one thought kept running through my mind: I had to find out the truth. And I would, no matter what it took.

CHAPTER
FOURTEEN

TRUTH IN THE SHADOWS

THERE WAS no use in going to visit the professor at eleven a.m. He wouldn't be home. After stewing in my bedroom for another ten minutes, I tromped down the stairs loud enough for Mom and Dad to hear me.

"Sera, come in here," Dad's said, his voice full of compassion.

"I heard everything," I confessed as I pushed open the study door. "Professor Theo…" a tear slipped down my cheek. Then I glanced around the study.

"Where are Sam, Isabella, and Josiah?"

"They are watching a movie," Mom said. "They're pretty upset as well."

"Lemon called. She and Jim are on their way over." Dad stood from his desk chair and walked toward the French doors of his study. "Lemon says she has some new evidence."

Mom and I followed Dad out of the study and down

the hall to the family room. "Will the evidence help the professor?" I asked, grasping for his hand.

He squeezed it. "I don't know, Sera. None of this makes sense."

He was right. None of it made sense. Even if one of Councilman Langston's relatives had murdered Professor Theo's great grandfather, why did that matter now? He couldn't be prosecuted, and why was it such a big deal who discovered the town?

"Dad, when someone names a town, do they get money?" I said testing a theory.

Dad patted me on the back. "No, sweetie. It's just an honor."

"Josiah is working on a report for homeschool group and it seems as if some people in the town have gotten richer while others have gotten nothing or poorer." I tried again.

Josiah rose from the sectional. "That's just economics, kiddo. I guess Mom and Dad told you about the professor." He frowned. "The professor may be a bit scatterbrained, but he's not crazy," he reassured me.

Sam pushed pause on the movie and Isabella motioned for me to join her on the sofa. Mom went to the kitchen to start a pot of coffee and get some snacks ready for Lemon and Agent Jim.

I sat next to Isabella and she leaned over and put her head on my shoulder. "They locked the professor up in the psychology ward."

I wasn't about to correct her. I let her cry on my shoulder until the doorbell chimed.

Dad raced down the hallway to answer the door. Rusty dashed into the family room, his paws making a clacking sound on the floor. Lemon and Agent Jim followed close behind. Lemon had this excited look on her face, and her bright pink lipstick seemed to shine even more in the light.

"You're not going to believe what I found out," Lemon said, almost breathless as she stopped right in front of Dad. She held up a small bag like it was the most important thing ever.

Dad looked up, his eyebrows going up in surprise. "What did you find?"

"There was a bullet hole in the skull of the skeleton," Lemon said, her eyes wide and her voice serious. She seemed kind of shaky, like she couldn't believe it herself.

Dad's face went all pale, and he whispered, "So he was murdered."

Rusty let out a low growl, like he knew something was wrong, and Lemon kept fiddling with her camera bag, making a soft rustling sound. It felt like the room got a lot heavier all of a sudden.

"That's not all," Lemon said. "I can't be sure, but the bullet could have come from a gun like the councilmen has on display in the Town Hall in a glass case."

"But what does that mean?" I said, shooting up from the couch. "No one can arrest the councilman for a murder committed so long ago."

"It's more than just pride, Sera. The councilman and the mayor have been using that false legacy to get rich. They've been making shady deals, maybe even committing crimes, all tied to the town's history. If Seamus Harrington is proven to be the true founder, they could lose everything—money, power, *everything*."

Mom joined us with a tray of muffins and coffee for the adults, and me, and hot chocolate for the rest of the kids. As we settled into our seats in the family room, Mom poured the coffee and Jim took over.

Jim took the coffee mug Mom handed him. "That had me puzzled as well, Sera. I've been digging into the journal, and other journals the professor has kept, and I found some information that will shake this town to the core."

Mom poured Lemon a cup of coffee and handed her the cream."What is it?"

"I can't be sure until I talk to the professor to clarify some of his notes, but it looks as if one of the reasons the councilman must maintain his status here, is he has some mob connections relying on it."

"Mob connections? Here? In Maplewood?" Sam said while he grabbed a muffin.

Lemon sipped her coffee. "And money laundering."

"The sudden influx of cash in the mayor's and councilman's pockets," Josiah said.

"What about the police?" Dad asked. "What is Bob doing?"

"I imagine, he is either on their payroll or they have something on him," Jim said.

"And all because I found a skeleton?" Isabella asked.

"No, this storm has been brewing in the town for a long time. The mayor just thought she and Victor could get away with it. The skeleton did trigger some memories for the professor and launched our investigation," Jim offered.

I stood and my muffin tumbled off my plate onto

the area rug. "So that's why they're so scared. They know if we find out the truth, they'll lose everything. But we can't just let them get away with it, right?"

A small smile tugs at the corner of Agent Jim's mouth. "That's why we're here, Sera. We're going to make sure the truth comes out, and they answer for what they've done."

"And get the professor out of the psych ward?" Mom asked.

I felt so helpless. Sure, I could uncover clues, but the rest – taking down the powerful mobsters and mayor weren't something I could do.

Lemon must have sensed my distress, because she wrapped her arm around me and said, "You're already a big part of this, Sera. You've got the instincts, just like Nancy Drew. We're going to crack this case wide open, and they won't see it coming."

CHAPTER
FIFTEEN

THE DARKEST HOUR

DAD AND JIM left for the hospital to talk to Professor Theo and see about getting him released. Lemon shared some more of her evidence with us and asked Josiah to see his research.

It was getting close to lunchtime and Mom said she was too upset to make something. Mom put in an order to The Sandwich Shop for sandwiches and The Cozy Corner Bookstore for pumpkin spice lattes for her and Lemon.

I asked if I could go with her to pick up the orders and grab Mandy on the way. Mom called Mandy's mom, and with permission for her to join us granted, she adjusted her online order.

Mom and I hopped in her Toyota van and headed downtown with a stop in Mandy's neighborhood. I was pretty quiet. I didn't know what else to say about the professor. Once Mandy was in the van, I filled her in on everything.

Her eyes grew wide with surprise and shock. "The police can grab people from their homes and lock them up?"

Mom clicked her turn signal and began backing out of Mandy's driveway.

She glanced over at me and said, "For evaluation, if friends and family members say the person has been acting as if they are exhibiting signs of mental health issues."

I leaned forward and placed my hand on the console between the front seats. "On second thought, Mom, can you drop us off at the park?"

Mom raised an eyebrow, examining me in the rearview mirror, "What for?"

I smiled and explained, "It's a nice fall day, and I want to fill Mandy in on everything."

Mom considered my request for a moment before nodding. "I suppose that's alright."

I reassured her, placing a hand on her arm. "We won't be in any danger, Mom."

Mom paused, tapping her finger against steering wheel. "How about I call Josiah and have him walk Isabella down to join you?"

I shook my head. "No. That's okay."

Her expression softened. "Sera, I've noticed you've been leaving her out a lot."

The weight of the case, the professor's evaluation, Officer Bob threatening us plus Isabella scooping me all the time was getting to me. A dam burst inside me and I yelled.

"Being a Nancy Drew sleuth was my thing and now she is noticing clues before me. She found the skeleton. That's my job," I yelled, banging my fists on the back of Mom's seat.

Mom pulled the van over to the Maplewood Community Park parking lot.

My body convulsed in as I sucked in a shuddering breath straining against my seatbelt. I turned to face the door, suddenly aware that I'd just had a raging meltdown in front of my best friend. The same sort of raging meltdown (as the therapist called them) that Isabella used to have on a daily basis. The same sort of meltdown that had gotten her kicked out of foster home after foster home, and an adoption terminated.

I jiggled the door handle and screamed, "Let me out!"

Mom popped the unlock button and I practically fell out of the car and hit the ground running. It didn't matter where. I crunched through a pile of dried up old leaves smelling of rot because they'd sat there too long. Tears blurred my vision as I ran to the base of the ancient oak tree where Isabella had found the skeleton and fell on my knees in the dirt.

A strong, warm hand pressed my back.

"It's okay, Sera," Mom said as she sank down beside me.

"You're going to send me back aren't you?" I sobbed.

"What? No. No. You're my daughter. My girl." she rubbed her hand in a circle.

A minute later, I'd calmed a bit and sat up. I looked

for Mandy. She was still in the van I guess, because I didn't see her anywhere.

"Sera, let's move over to the pavilion and talk."

"What about the sandwiches and coffees?"

"I called Robin at The Sandwich Shop and she's going to deliver both." Mom helped me to my feet. "But that's not important right now."

I glanced down at my muddy knees and my eye caught something in the dirt. Something gold. I fell back to my knees and dug around the edges.

"What did you find, Sera?" Mandy yelled as she ran across the park.

Mom joined me on the ground and dug with me. Then I remembered what Lemon had said about disturbing the evidence. "Stop, Mom! We need to call Lemon."

A shadow moved over us, blocking the sun. "No, you don't."

"Councilman," Mom put a hand on her knee and turned toward him.

Councilman Langston's salt-and-pepper hair, a neatly trimmed beard, and piercing gray eyes blended in well with the shadow he had created. His gray tailored suit was a stark contrast to our muddy hands and clothing. His stern expression and the gun he was holding froze me in my tracks.

"Don't stop, Sera, dig it up," and he pivoted around and pointed the gun at Mandy. "Or I shoot your little friend." He motioned for Mandy to join us under the oak tree.

Mom dug furiously. "Let the kids go, Victor."

"I don't think so. These kids as you call them have

almost ruined my life. But that stops now."

Mom unearthed the medallion, it was only a couple inches wide. As Mom dusted the dirt off, I couldn't help but say, "It's Professor Theo's family crest."

Mom handed the muddied medallion to the councilman's outstretched hand.

"Now move." The councilman waved his gun, motioning toward the huge grave that once held the skeleton of Professor Theo's great grandfather. He had a crazed look in his eyes.

He cackled. "Looks as if your grave is dug for you."

What would Nancy Drew do in a situation like this? She always got away even if the situation seemed impossible. I'd been shot before, my arm was grazed by a bullet really. I didn't want to get shot again. More importantly, I didn't want Mandy and Mom to suffer because of me. And I didn't want the councilman to get away with Professor Theo's medallion and him to be locked up forever in the psych ward.

Mom's car alarm blared and the councilman turned to see where the sound was coming from. It was long enough for Mom to grab a large branch and swing it, knocking the gun out of his hands. "Run, girls!"

Mandy and I scrambled out of the grave and I dragged her by the arm to the pavilion. I stopped short and I turned to check on Mom. She held the gun in her hand and her phone in the other.

"Put both your hands on your head," a stern voice ordered from behind the oak tree. Agent Jim Gains stepped out from behind the tree, his flaming red hair standing on end. Three FBI agents, clad in black tactical gear stormed into the park. They swiftly apprehended the startled councilman, who barely had time to react before he was cuffed and secured.

Mandy and I clung to each other, our breaths coming in ragged gasps as we watched the FBI agents drag the councilman away. Mom ran over and pulled us both into a tight embrace, her hands trembling as she held us close.

Just then, Professor Theo hurried over, his wild white hair more disheveled than usual. He kneeled beside the hole we had just escaped from, his sharp eyes narrowing as he spotted the medallion in the dirt. His fingers trembled as he picked it up, brushing off the mud to reveal the familiar design.

"My family crest," he whispered, his voice a mix of awe and sorrow. "After all these years…"

Mom nodded, her eyes brimming with unshed tears. "We did it, Sera. We uncovered the truth."

The professor looked up at us, his expression softening as he clutched the medallion to his chest. "Thanks to you, my family's name can finally be restored."

I glanced back at the spot where the medallion had been buried by the councilman. The weight of the secrets buried beneath us had finally been lifted, and the shadows that once loomed over Maplewood Community Park seemed to dissolve in the warm afternoon light.

The sound of approaching sirens filled the air, and as I looked at Professor Theo's grateful smile, I knew this chapter of our lives was closing. The truth had come to light, and with it, the hope for a new beginning.

CHAPTER
SIXTEEN

A HALLOWEEN TO REMEMBER

THE COOL OCTOBER air carried the scent of fallen leaves and the crispness of a fall evening as Maplewood Community Park buzzed with excitement. The park was strewn with vibrant orange lights draped across the ancient oak tree's sprawling branches, casting long shadows in the fading evening light. The town had "pulled out all the stops" Dad said, with carved pumpkins lining the walkways, their flickering candles casting eerie yet inviting glows on the ground below.

With the mayor and Councilman Victor Langston in jail, the festivities that day were in honor of Seamus Harrington. Professor Theo presided over the party as townspeople congregated. Agent Jim Gains and his team of FBI agents had worked long into the night sifting through the evidence at Mayor Evelyn Harper's office and the home of Victor Langston. I only knew that because Lemon told me. Dad and Mom had assured me that the grown-ups were handling it and I should enjoy the party.

Lemon dressed as Amelia Earhart for the Halloween party. She wore a vintage-style brown leather aviator jacket, the kind that seemed to have been through many daring adventures, paired with matching brown trousers tucked into sturdy, knee-high lace-up boots. A white silk scarf was loosely knotted around her neck, fluttering slightly as she moved, evoking the image of Amelia in the cockpit of her plane. Her hair, usually styled in Marilyn-esque curls, was tucked under a brown leather aviator cap, complete with vintage goggles perched on her forehead.

Lemon's bright lipstick was still there. She carried a small, leather satchel slung over her shoulder, adding to the authenticity of the look.

Rusty, her faithful dog, was dressed to match, donning a mini aviator jacket of his own, complete with a tiny pair of goggles that rested on his furry head.

Professor Theo Harrington stood near the edge of the Halloween festivities at Maplewood Community Park, his presence unmistakable among the crowd. His wild, white hair was as unruly as ever, giving him the air of an eccentric genius. That night, he had opted for a suit that was both festive and a bit peculiar—a deep black jacket adorned with tiny, intricate skeleton patterns, perfectly fitting for the occasion.

Around his neck, he wore a bow tie that featured a similar skeletal design, its bright orange color popping against the dark fabric of his suit. But the piece that truly caught everyone's eye was the family crest he had pinned to his lapel, a small but ornate emblem that had been unearthed just days earlier along with the skeleton.

As the children ran around enjoying the party, Professor Harrington stood smiling with pride, a bridge between the past and the present, his attire reflecting both the celebration of the season and the weight of his family's history.

I glanced at Isabella and couldn't help but smile. She was rocking the whole math teacher vibe, complete with a pencil tucked behind her ear and a pair of over-sized glasses perched on her nose. Her hair was pulled back into a neat bun, and she wore a cardigan that looked like something straight out of a 1950s classroom. The outfit was simple but perfect—Isabella totally nailed it. It was hard to believe we'd been at odds not too long ago. Now, here we were, mending fences and moving through the crowd like old friends.

As for me, I was channeling my inner Miss Marple. My costume was an old-fashioned dress with a lace collar, a cardigan draped over my shoulders, and a string of pearls around my neck. I even managed to find a hat that screamed "quaint English village." I clutched my handbag like it held all of Miss Marple's secrets, feeling like I could solve any mystery that came my way. The best part? Isabella noticed. She gave me a nod of approval, and I felt a little burst of pride. We might have had our differences, but tonight, we were on the same team.

Mom and I had talked the evening after my melt-down and near-death experience in the park. Mom had assured me that it was okay to be angry and not try to be the nice one all the time. It turned out Isabella wasn't trying to "steal my show," as Mom had put it. She was finding her gifts and talents, and I should support her. Her math skills and eye for detail were a complement to my sleuthing. Plus, Mom assured me it was okay to be a kid sometimes and just have fun without being Nancy Drew.

We carried bags filled with candy, barely able to contain our excitement as we joined Mandy. Mandy, in her professor get-up and a silver Einstein wig, skipped ahead of the group, her fair skin glowing under the park's string lights. She paused to adjust her bow tie and round spectacles, laughing as she spun around, her blue eyes sparkling with the evening's energy.

Sam was dressed as Alexander Hamilton for the Halloween party, complete with a ruffled shirt, knee-length breeches, and a tricorn hat. His costume was a nod to his love for history, and he proudly carried a replica quill pen tucked into his vest, adding an extra touch of authenticity to his outfit.

Mom and Dad mingled with the other grown-ups, including Mandy's parents who had thanked Mom repeatedly for saving their daughter.

Josiah was dressed as George Washington for the Halloween party. He wore a blue military-style coat with gold trim, a white wig to mimic Washington's hairstyle, and tall black boots. He even carried a replica sword at his side, completing the look of the revered American general and first president.

I noticed Louisa and Edmund immediately—they were hard to miss with their flaming red hair, just like their dad's. Louisa was dressed as a fairy-tale princess, but not the frilly, glittery kind. Her dress was a deep forest green, with golden embroidery along the edges, and she wore a crown of autumn leaves and tiny acorns. She looked like she had just stepped out of an enchanted forest, and even though she was younger than me, I couldn't help but admire the attention to detail in her costume.

Edmund, on the other hand, was all about action. He was decked out as a brave knight, complete with a shiny silver helmet that was just a bit too big for his head. His armor was made of foam but looked almost real, especially in the dim light of the party. A bright red cape flowed behind him, matching his fiery hair, and he carried a plastic sword that he brandished with more enthusiasm than skill. He looked like he was ready to take on any dragon—or maybe just chase his sister around the party.

It was clear they had put a lot of thought into their costumes, and seeing them so excited made me smile. They were just like their dad, Agent Jim—full of energy and spirit.

After everything that went down at the Town Hall meeting, I thought people would be mad at us forever. Everyone was so angry, yelling about how unsafe the town was and freaking out over the skeleton in the park. It felt like the walls were closing in that night, and I was trying my hardest not to lose it. But now, just a few days later, things were totally different.

As I walked through the park with Isabella, Mandy, and Sam, I noticed people looking at us—not with fear or frustration like before, but almost like they respected us. The first person to come over was Mrs. Thompson, the lady who had been so upset at the meeting, saying the park wasn't safe anymore.

She smiled at me, kind of shy. "Sera," she said, her voice way softer than it had been before, "I owe you an apology. I was so scared that night, I didn't stop to think about what you and your friends had really done. You uncovered the truth and protected this town from those terrible people. Thank you."

My face felt warm, but I wasn't one to shy away. "We just followed the clues," I said confidently, like I always told Isabella and Mandy. "That's what any good detective would do."

Before I could say anything else, Mr. Daniels, the guy who had stood up and yelled about us digging at the crime scene, came over. "You kids," he said, shaking his head with a small laugh, "you did what none of us could do. I was wrong to doubt you. You saved this town from the mayor and Councilman Langston's schemes, and you've got my respect for that."

Isabella nudged me, grinning, but I was already stepping forward to say more. "It was a team effort, though," I added, glancing at my friends. "We couldn't have done it without working together."

Just then, Ms. Davidson, the new mayor who took over after they arrested Mayor Evelyn Harper, walked up to us. "I wanted to thank you all personally," she said, her voice warm and sincere. "Exposing Councilman Langston's lies about his family founding the town, and uncovering the mob money that was used to build his and Mayor Harper's fortunes—that took real courage. You've done this town a great service, and we're all incredibly proud of you."

I stood a little taller, feeling like I'd really made a difference. "We just had to find the truth," I said, determined. "It's what we do."

Ms. Davidson nodded, looking serious. "You reminded us all how important it is to stand up for the truth. Thanks to you, this town can finally move forward."

As more people came over, thanking us and apologizing, I felt a weird mix of pride and relief. It wasn't just about solving the mystery anymore—it was about helping our town heal and move forward. I glanced at my friends, knowing we'd always remember this moment, not just for what we uncovered, but for how it brought us all together.

Isabella, Sam, Mandy, and I made a beeline for the food tables as soon as we got the chance. The smell of sandwiches hit us first, and my stomach growled. The Sandwich Shop had sent over a ton of different kinds—there were turkey and Swiss ones that looked so good, and some with roast beef that had a spicy mustard spread. Sam grabbed a veggie wrap, and Mandy followed suit, while Isabella and I loaded our plates with anything that looked tasty. The sandwiches were all cut into neat triangles, so it was easy to try a little of everything without feeling too stuffed.

But the real showstopper was the Bea's Bakery table. Mandy's eyes went wide when she saw the massive cake in the center. It was a spice cake with thick cream cheese frosting, and it looked almost too pretty to eat, with marzipan leaves in all sorts of fall colors. We each grabbed a cupcake—mine had orange frosting with a candy corn on top, and Sam's was covered in chocolate sprinkles. Isabella snagged a pumpkin-shaped cookie, and Mandy picked out one of the powdered sugar ones. It was like a dessert dream come true.

After piling our plates high, we headed over to the drink station, which was surrounded by people holding steaming cups. The Cozy Corner had brought over giant dispensers filled with coffee and hot chocolate. Sam wrinkled his nose at the coffee, but the rest of us couldn't resist the hot chocolate. It was rich and creamy, with marshmallows bobbing on top. They even had bottles of flavored syrups, so I added a squirt of caramel to mine, while Mandy and Isabella went for peppermint.

We found a spot near the edge of the crowd and settled down with our feast. The food was amazing, and the hot chocolate was perfect for the chilly night. As we dug in, laughing and comparing notes on what we liked best, I couldn't help but feel like this party was turning out to be pretty awesome, especially with all of us together.

The party was in full swing, with the town's residents milling about, enjoying the festivities. The scent of chocolate and pumpkin cookies filled the air as laughter and chatter echoed through the park. Amid the joy and excitement was the anticipation of the ceremony for the real town's founder, Seamus Harrington.

As we gathered near the oak tree, our thoughts turned back to the mysterious skeleton and the unsettling events that had unfolded in the days leading up to the party.

Professor Theo Harrington, standing before the gathered townsfolk at Maplewood Community Park, took a deep breath, his wild hair catching the flickering light of the lanterns. With a gentle touch on the family crest pinned to his lapel, he began to speak, his voice a mix of pride and emotion.

"Ladies and gentlemen, friends, and neighbors, tonight we stand on the threshold of history, not just to celebrate Halloween, but to honor the truth that has long been buried—both in our town's past and quite literally beneath our feet. For years, our town's origins have been shrouded in mystery, a puzzle that has finally found its missing piece. That piece is my great grandfather, Seamus Harrington.

Seamus was a man of great vision, though history has not always been kind in preserving the legacies of men like him. He was a founder in the truest sense, a man who laid the very foundation upon which this community was built. Tonight, we do more than just recognize his contributions—we reclaim his rightful place in our town's history.

This acknowledgment is not just for him, but for all those who came before us, who worked, lived, and dreamed of a town where we could gather as we do now. It is a moment of justice, of truth, and of pride for the Harrington family, and for this town we all cherish.

May we move forward with the understanding that history is not just about the past—it's a living, breathing force that shapes who we are today. Thank you for joining me on this momentous occasion, and for embracing the truth of our town's origins. Together, we can honor the past while building a brighter future for Maplewood."

As he concluded, a ripple of applause filled the

park, the town finally embracing the true founder of Maplewood and the legacy he left behind.

In the front row, Isabella, Sam, Mandy, Josiah, and I exchanged excited glances, our eyes wide with the realization that we had played a part in uncovering this piece of history. We nudged each other with grins, the weight of the mystery we'd unraveled finally sinking in.

Nearby, Professor Harrington's long-time housekeeper, Mrs. Eliza Wainwright, stood with a proud smile, her hands clasped tightly in front of her. She had known the professor's family history for years, tending to him and his home with steady loyalty. That night, she dabbed at her eyes with a handkerchief, watching her employer and friend finally receive the recognition his family deserved.

As the party picked up again after the speech, I noticed Agent Jim and his wife, Kat, making their way over. They had Louisa and Edmund in tow, the kids still bouncing with excitement. As they got closer, the kids each with a cupcake in hand, ran behind a clump of maple trees to play. Jim caught my eye and gave me one of his rare, small smiles—a smile that made him look a little less like a skeleton and more like a proud dad.

"Well, well," Jim said, his voice gruff but warm. "Looks like we've got some real detectives in the making." He patted us each on the back awkwardly with a pumpkin-sized hand sending us reeling forward.

As we righted ourselves, Kat nodded and laughed grasping me by the arm to steady me. "You girls did an amazing job," she added, her eyes sparkling. "You may be just girl detectives, but you can solve any case."

"Thank you," I replied my heart melting because she quoted Nancy Drew. Kat was famous for quoting murder mysteries and I felt special because she quoted one with us. We really were the three sleuths. Just like Nancy Drew!

Louisa shot out from the tree she was hiding behind and bulldozed into Kat's legs. Kat reached down and patted her on the back before continuing, "It's not every day that kids solve a mystery like this. You must be so proud of yourselves."

I felt my face heat up, and I glanced at Isabella and Mandy, who were standing beside me, looking just as embarrassed and pleased as I was. "We just followed the clues," I mumbled, trying to sound modest even though my heart was swelling with pride.

"Following clues is what good detectives do," Jim stated, his tone serious. "You kept your heads cool, asked the right questions, and didn't give up—even when things got tough. That's not something just anyone can do."

Kat smiled at me and turned to wipe Louisa's icing-smeared face with a baby wipe she'd pulled out of her purse. "And you all worked together. That's what made the difference. You're a great team."

I exchanged a glance with Isabella and Mandy. It felt good to hear that, especially after everything we'd been through. "Thanks," I said quietly. I smoothed my dress and played with my string of pearls. "It wasn't easy, but we stuck it out."

Jim nodded approvingly. "That's what counts. You should be proud."

Kat leaned in closer, her voice lowering to a whisper.

"And I have to say, your costumes are fantastic. Perfect for the occasion."

I laughed, the tension easing as I looked down at my Miss Marple outfit. "Thanks. We figured we might as well dress the part."

"You did more than that," Jim said, his eyes twinkling. "You solved the case. That's something to celebrate."

With that, he gave us a rare, genuine smile—a smile that made me feel like maybe, just maybe, we were as good as he said we were.

———

Read next:

The Case Of The Missing Heirloom: A Nancy Drew-Inspired Adventure

ABOUT THE AUTHOR

Kathleen Guire is the mother of seven, four through adoption, NiNi of fourteen, former National Parent of the Year, author, teacher, and speaker. She loves connecting with readers through her website (Kathleen guireauthor.com).

For more information,
about Kathleen, check out her website and follow her
on social media!
www.kathleenguireauthor.com
kathleenguire@gmail.com
https://linktr.ee/kguire

ALSO BY KATHLEEN GUIRE

Made in the USA
Columbia, SC
20 November 2024

46753256R00075